CRADLE OF HOPE

HANNAH SCHROCK

CHAPTER 1

*J*udith Miller was sure God had answered their prayers. Her body's rhythms followed a predictable pattern and yet throughout the three years of her marriage to Isaac, she had struggled to conceive. Not due to lack of trying. At first, they had laughed about her inability to fall pregnant.

Isaac tickled her tummy, cuddling in the dark of the night, and peered at his wife with a mischievous smile.

"Maybe you haven't fallen pregnant yet because the baby knows I might be jealous to share my affection."

Judith laughed. She snuggled closer to her

broad-shouldered, long-limbed husband, with eyes the color of sky after summer rains. She nudged his side and he turned his head to kiss her forehead. His hand moved lazily, caressing her shoulder, before trailing to her face and she squirmed, smiling.

Isaac's eyes focused on hers, his gaze indulgent. "I'll make *kaffe* this morning."

"*Danke*. But not so quick."

His eyes widened. " I have planting to do. Much as I would like to slack off and spend more time with you"

Judith giggled. "That can wait five minutes. You had better get used to sharing my affection."

He gave her an incredulous grin. "Are you telling me what I think?"

"Uh-huh. My monthly cycle is ten days late. I feel different too."

He drew himself up, leaning against the headboard to stare at her. Judith pulled herself up, her cinnamon-colored hair tangled and falling to her waist.

"Are you sure?"

"As sure as the sun rises every day."

His arms wrapped around her in a bear hug, his

face nestled against hers. "Aw, *Lieb*. That is *Wunderbar* news! *Danke*."

Judith whispered, "I am so excited!" She had already thanked Gott that she had fallen pregnant after she counted the days on the calendar the previous evening.

Isaac gazed at her, his eyes dreamy. "Me, too. I am thankful our prayers have been answered."

She nodded. "So thankful."

Isaac patted her shoulder. "You think of baby names while I make us *kaffe*."

Judith laughed. "I already did."

"Tell me."

She kissed him lightly. "Later. I need the bathroom." She got out of the bed and felt her husband's eyes on her. He was standing on the other side of the bed, staring at her as if fixed to the spot.

"What?" she asked, at the thought of a baby growing inside her. Their firstborn.

"I want to remember this moment. I love you."

"I love you, too." Isaac was an introvert and yet Judith had never felt as loved by anyone. He had a knack for saying the right words when she needed them. Whether words of encouragement, love, or praise. When he scolded her, which was seldom, he was gentle and fair.

Isaac shook his head, grinning. "We're going to have a *boppli*! See you in the kitchen." He left the bedroom with a spring in his step. At twenty-five years old and already married three years, Judith was late to fall pregnant in comparison with her friends. They had all assured her that she would fall pregnant when it was Gott's will.

But Judith had battled with doubt and disappointment in recent months. She had feared she might never conceive. Now she had reason to to be thankful. Only her faith in Gott and His broader plan had kept her praying. And Isaac's insistence that they not give in to fear of the Enemy. Now her faith had been restored. *Please forgive me for wavering in my faith at times.*

As a vegetable farmer, Isaac was known in Lancaster county for his faith. He had planted his usual crop the year before despite the harsh drought. Many other Amish farmers were dumbfounded by his bumper crop. Many of them had planted fewer crops, thinking it was a waste of seeds and labor to plant more when they were expecting low rainfall again.

Much of their crop had withered in the heat,

without the usual rains. At one stage, Isaac's fields had looked like they would suffer the same fate. Then one evening's steady rain restored his fields and fortunes. His farm enjoyed the best harvest he had ever had. His success was even more remarkable in a drought year, without fancy irrigation methods. When other farmers asked his secret, he always gave the same answer.

"God is our Provider. He is faithful." Then he'd lean towards them. "It helps to get on your knees. Tell Him your troubles when you're buckling under the pressure. His yoke is light. Besides, we don't want to bother our wives with our troubles."

The first time Judith heard that, she saved her comment until later, when they got home. "Maybe we also had more rain than they did."

Isaac shrugged. "Maybe. Trusting in *Gott's* provision sure beats feeling defeated."

"I wish I had half your faith," Judith murmured. "I struggle to believe at times."

Isaac tilted his head to look at her. "I reckon you've got more faith than you think."

"What makes you say that?"

He grinned. "You married me, for one. You know how obstinate I am. You still married me."

Judith threw her head back and laughed. "You

have a point there." Her green eyes softened. "I'm glad I married you."

"I thank *Gott* you did!" Isaac picked her up, his arms firmly around her waist, right there, in the middle of the cornfield. He twirled her around, her feet several inches above the ground, her rosy cheeks catching the sun.

Now, as Judith dressed, she wondered how many more months she could get away with wearing her dresses before she needed new ones. She'd ask her mother, Sadie Yoder later after she announced the happy news. While Sadie was already a grandmother, Judith was sure she would be ecstatic after many months of worrying.

Judith's older brother, Mark, was a year older than her and married to Ruby. They had a boy and a girl, Charlie and Hannah, aged three and one year respectively. There was never a dull moment in their household. Charlie's latest escapade was drawing a heart on his baby sister's bedroom wall. While annoyed at the mess he'd made with the wax crayon, Ruby sorted out the situation with her usual calmness.

"You wipe that off the wall, Mister," Ruby ordered, handing him a soapy rag.

His mouth trembled. "Sorry, *Mamm*."

"Then clean it up."

Charlie glowered at her. He set to work immediately, first giving one hesitant wipe of the wall. Ruby didn't tolerate nonsense.

"Give me that."

He handed her the damp cloth, his bottom lip stuck out, reminding her he was a rebellious three-year-old.

Judith wiped his artwork, smearing it. "Like this. Needs elbow grease to get it off properly. Why did you think I was so cross, rascal?" She handed the cloth back, watching him.

Charlie pressed the cloth to the wall as if his life depended on it. Ruby smiled as she watched his efforts, her anger gone. He managed to get most of the crayon marks off after concerted rubbing.

Ruby hugged him. "*Gut* job cleaning that up. I forgive you. Please don't do that again."

Besides a sister-in-law, Judith also had a younger sister, May. Only twenty years old, she was unmarried. May still lived with Judith's parents, Ben and Sadie Yoder. *May would be excited at becoming an aunt again.* Judith joined Isaac in the kitchen.

He smiled, handing her a mug imprinted with

the word Lancaster. "Just in time." Isaac clinked his mug gently against hers. "Congratulations to us, clever parents!"

"Congratulations!"

"Now tell me what names you've thought of."

Judith took a sip of coffee before answering. "If we have a boy, let's call him Ben, after my father. If we have a girl, how about Ruth?"

"I like both names. Your *daed* will be pleased."

She stared at her coffee. "One of my friends felt sick at the smell of *kaffe* when she was pregnant. Didn't drink it most of her pregnancy."

"Hopefully that doesn't happen to you. Everyone is different."

"You're probably right. It's too soon to have morning sickness yet. Hopefully, I don't suffer with that either."

Isaac touched her cheek briefly. "Whatever happens, I'll be with you every step of the way."

"I will need new dresses."

"Of course. Order some in the meantime."

"*Danke.*"

"When are you telling your parents?"

"On Sunday. We're having lunch with them, remember?"

Isaac nodded. "Are Mark and Ruby going too?"

"My *mamm* didn't mention it, so I doubt it. I will whisper in their ears at church. They can keep a secret. *Mamm* will want to tell the whole world once she knows."

Isaac wrapped an arm around Judith's shoulder. "She's going to be happy."

"*Jah*! She tried not to show it but she was getting worried."

Isaac grinned. "*Boppli* on the way or or not, your kisses are always heavenly."

Judith smiled flirtatiously. "Better kiss me again before the *boppli* arrives."

He chuckled. "Better save that for later. I need to start that planting." He glanced outside. "Going to be a scorcher today."

"I will pack homemade lemonade."

"*Danke*. That will be appreciated."

Judith could tell by the distracted look in her husband's eyes that his mind was on the tasks he had lined up. She wouldn't have it any other way. She was proud of his success as a farmer. They were a team. She helped to farm the cash produce that they sold at the markets near their community.

Isaac's gaze returned to Judith as she started cooking their breakfast. "I forgot to ask with all the excitement. When is our baby due?"

"Winter. In early January."

"That's thoughtful of the *boppli*."

Confused, Judith stared at him. "What is?"

"The mornings will start getting warmer then. Easier for you to feed him." Isaac grinned. "Or her."

"I hadn't thought that far ahead."

"Us farmers, we're always planning."

Judith blinked. "I just thought of something. Are you happy for me to have the baby at home?"

"Wouldn't want it any other way," Isaac said quietly. "Why are you asking that now?"

Judith giggled. "Planning, like my husband taught me."

"Touche! Is there time for me to have a shower before breakfast?"

"Sure. I'll keep your breakfast warm."

Isaac planted a kiss on her forehead like he did when he wanted her to know he was pleased. "See you in a bit."

THE NEXT FEW months passed quickly, the young couple in a whirl of activity as they coordinated their schedules to get the utmost return on their efforts. They frequented the local markets, selling the fresh produce from their farm.

"We did much better than last August," Judith remarked, tapping the ledger book with her pen.

"*Jah*, I noticed sales were up considerably on some vegetables." Isaac studied her. "Must be that extra farmer's market we added to our list."

"*Jah*, that helped. But we also got a lot of orders from several hotels. Remember, we signed them up earlier this year? Their guests prefer vegetables free of pesticides. We've done very well."

Judith put her pen down, rubbing her neck. She sighed, glad to be finished with the month's accounts. She was good at recording expenses and income but she found month-end stressful. Only because she respected the importance of doing an excellent job.

Isaac put down the crate he was getting ready to stack with another crop of corn. "How much better did we do over last year?"

"Guess!" Judith's green eyes brightened with glee.

He pressed a hand to his chin as he considered. "Up ten percent?"

"Guess again."

"More than that?"

"Much more."

He shook his head. "You tell me."

"Sales are up twenty percent."

"You're kidding!" He grinned. "I think we should take Friday afternoon off. Have a picnic."

Judith covered her mouth as she yawned. "I like the sound of that."

Isaac stood behind her chair, massaging the tight knots near her shoulders. "I'm proud of you, Judith. I wouldn't have achieved those results by myself. You brought in those hotels."

"Ah, that feels *gut*."

Isaac laughed. "Did you hear what I said?"

She turned her head, smiling at him. "Uh-huh. But you're the one who managed to produce another bumper crop."

He grinned. "Thankfully. And we have a *boppli* on the way. That's the best news of all!"

Judith stretched a hand upwards to meet his. "We are blessed."

Isaac squeezed her hand in return. "*Jah*, we are."

A FEW DAYS LATER, keen to get their chores done for the day so they could go on their picnic, Isaac carried a customer's purchases to her car in the parking area. The customer's little girl who was only about four, ran out in front of a passing car. Isaac dropped the box he was carrying, making a clunk. He ran into the road, pushing the child out of the way of the speeding car.

Judith frowned as she heard a car's horn and tires screeching to a standstill. Then a woman's screams, followed by shouting from what sounded like several people. A car door slammed. Anxious to provide help, she hurriedly left their stall and headed in the direction of the commotion. She walked towards the parking lot, looking out frantically for Isaac.

Her face went pale as she saw him, crumpled and broken on the tarmac, groaning. He was in so much pain, she wondered if he comprehended the crowd gathered around him.

"I'm his wife," Judith said urgently, kneeling beside Isaac.

"I've called an ambulance," an ashen-faced man said. "I was driving the car. I'm so sorry."

"He didn't have time to stop," a woman said, taking his hand. "A little girl ran out in front of our car. Your husband pushed her out of the way and our car hit him. We couldn't help it."

Judith nodded, everything a blur of tears and urgent voices. Later, she sat by Isaac's side in the ambulance. The following week was the worst of her life. She spent every day at the hospital until finally a doctor approached her.

"Mrs. Miller. We did everything we could to try to save your husband." His voice was ragged from lack of sleep and heavy. "I'm sorry for your loss. Isaac has passed." Judith stared at him. Empty of thought. Her chest filled with an ache so sharp she gasped for breath.

"No!" she exclaimed. She saw compassion in the doctor's eyes. *Nothing would bring Isaac back.*

ISAIAH WAS BORN PREMATURELY four months later – a month before his due date. Judith heard his hearty cries as he took his first gulps of air.

"Your baby is strong," the nurse said, peering at Judith with concern. Her forehead was damp with sweat.

"*Hallo*, Isaiah," Judith murmured as the nurse placed the blanket-wrapped bundle in her arms. Judith tilted her neck, to gaze in wonder at her dark-haired son. Was it her fault that he was born early? She was so stressed after losing Isaac and running the farm alone after burying him. Her brother, Mark was helping out where he could, but he had his job and family.

Isaiah's little hand clutched Judith's fingers. *She had to be strong for him.*

CHAPTER 2

Two years later, Judith was no closer to finding a solution to managing the farm. As she took her seat in the barn for the bimonthly church service, Judith gave the women seated on either side of her a tight smile. She had kept the farm sustainable for two years. She wasn't going to give up on it now. The only blessing in all this was Isaiah.

If only Isaac was alive to share the joys of raising their son.

Judith was so exhausted that sleep seemed the greatest reward in a life made up of farming, and managing orders and accounts. Taking care of Isaiah was her highest priority. Yet she felt guilty at not being able to spend a full day with him. She was missing out on milestones. The first time he had gurgled and smiled, he had been at her mother when he was four months old.

Sadie, Judith's mother, pressed a comforting arm on her shoulder after she told her Isaiah smiled for the first time that morning.

"Isaiah loves you. He knows you're his *mamm*."

Judith nodded. "*Danke, Mamm.*" She picked up her baby son, appreciating the gurgle he gave her. Yet, rather than being happy, she had that familiar sharp ache of loss that seldom went away. This time, the loss was for the hours that she wasn't spending with her toddler. *Was she selfish, wanting that?*

"*Mamm!*" Isaiah said with a follow-up smile, keen to attract his mother's attention after being away from her that morning. Judith and Isaiah had developed a steady, reliable routine. Every weekday, Judith took the buggy to her parents' home so her mother could mind Isaiah, with him seated at her side, cheerful on most days. Often chattering so much that she could scarcely get a word in edgeways.

Judith soaked up the journey to her mother's in the mornings. Every moment spent with her son was precious. An opportunity to bond with him.

Nurture him. Experience his progress. *He hadn't known his father, so he couldn't miss him.*

Isaiah was spending this Sunday morning with his cousins, Charlie and Hannah, while Judith attended the church service. She found it hard to believe that Charlie was five now. Three-year-old Hannah was only a year older than Isaiah. She enjoyed bossing her younger cousin around occasionally until her mother Ruby stepped in, saving the situation from escalating.

Hannah was sweet to Isaiah on most days but, being toddlers, they sometimes vyed for attention. Martha, a friend of Judith's, had raised the idea that week of her courting again. Judith stared at her in alarm.

"I'm not ready."

Martha nodded, her eyes gentle. "I only suggested that because I care about you."

"I know you do. *Danke*, Martha. You're a *gut* friend." *Please drop the topic.*

"I just want to say one more thing," Martha said cautiously.

"What's that?" Judith smiled, conscious that her friend was brave enough to raise the topic, being that she was her closest friend.

"If you courted and got married again, your life would be easier. I can see how tired you are."

"Ask any mother of a two-year-old if she is tired," Judith said, aware that her flippant tone was an attempt to disguise her heartache.

"True." Martha sighed. "But you're lonely. I can see it in your eyes."

Judith's blue eyes were stubborn. "I've got friends." Martha studied her with an expression that told Judith she didn't believe she was fine.

"Just think about courting."

She might as well get this out of the way. "Okay, if I decided to court, what *mann* would be interested in a widow with a boisterous two-year-old in tow?"

"Now you're being silly. You'd get a babysitter."

"Makes a pleasant change being silly," Judith mumbled.

Martha gave her a stern look. "If you court again, I could babysit Isaiah now and again."

Judith nudged her friend's arm, her bleak mood lifting at the possibility of being carefree again. "Could I get that offer in writing please?"

Martha laughed. "It's good to see you smiling again."

Her sweet comment touched Judith's heart. "I

love Isaiah. If I ever courted again, I would have to be careful. I wouldn't want him to be disappointed if things didn't work out."

"You don't need Isaiah's permission to go courting." Martha's eyes contained a twinkle.

Judith's mouth twitched. "Do I still need my father's?"

"Probably," Martha said dryly. They burst into laughter. Wiping her eyes afterward, Judith stared at her friend.

"Right now, I need a farm manager more than being asked whether I'd like to go courting."

Martha's gray eyes registered surprise. "I thought your *bruder* was helping you."

"Mark is helping a lot. But he is taking strain. He's got his business to run and a *familye* of his own."

Martha frowned. "I see."

"Mark and my sister-in-law, Ruby have been amazing. Ruby helps with babysitting when my mother can't. I don't want to put further strain on Mark's marriage. It's not fair to expect him to constantly be helping me with the farm."

"What are you going to do then?"

"I haven't got a clue." Judith looked at her friend fiercely. "I'm keeping the farm. No question about that. I'm sure Isaac would have wanted that. And I love farming." She gave a heavy sigh. "I just need an extra pair of hands."

Judith struggled to concentrate during the church service. Not just from lack of sleep but worry. Her mind kept on returning to her struggle to keep on top of all the work that needed doing. Soon, she'd be entering the busiest period. The period just before Christmas was nonstop with packing orders for the regular customers at the farmer's markets.

The hotels had all increased their orders. News was, they were expecting a busy season despite the snowy Christmas that many folk were predicting. The young widow didn't know what to do. She came back to the present with a start as the congregation rose to sing a hymn. She concentrated on the words, relieved to throw off her worries as she joined neighbors and friends in singing. The words gave her comfort, reminding her of the brotherhood of man.

Reminding her that God ruled over them all. The congregation was made up of the households of about thirty neighboring farms and their related families. Most of the people singing around her had known her since childhood. They knew her joys and sorrows. While she never complained, there was comfort in not pretending all was well. Just being thankful for her community's company. And remembering to thank Gott for mercies.

She hadn't seen Mark when she arrived that morning. She had struggled to rouse Charlie from his bed that morning. He had been fretful during the night, complaining of a tummy ache. She had a suspicion he had eaten more candy than was good for him when he visited her mother on Saturday. Judith had to tell her not to indulge Isaiah when he asked for more candy. She suffered the consequences whenever Isaiah ate sugary treats.

Judith was strict in that regard. Her mother doted on her grandchildren and she had made them all toffee apples. She didn't mind her giving Isaiah the occasional treat, but he had looked decidedly green last night. At one stage she thought he was going to throw up. Judith eventually saved the situation by letting Isaiah climb into her bed. He fell asleep soon afterward, content to be close to his mother.

Isaiah looked so angelic and peaceful that Judith's heart had filled with joy. Cherishing her lift in mood, she stayed awake a while longer. She struggled to wake up in the morning, wishing she could have slept another hour. Now that she was at church, she felt restored in hope again. Stronger. Although she was still so tired that, if she had rested her head on someone's shoulder, she would have fallen asleep.

What a thought!

The church service was eventually over, and Judith followed the line of women slowly making their way out of the barn towards the trestle tables set up outside where the families would enjoy lunch together. They each brought an offering for the table. That way, there was enough for all and a good selection of food to choose from. Gathering after the church service was the highlight of Judith's week. She seldom met up with friends these days, besides chatting with them at church twice a month. There weren't enough hours in the day.

How would she ever fit in courting as well? Judith's face lit up as Mark strolled towards her. He kissed her cheek.

"Morning. You are looking better today."

She gave a wry laugh. "*Danke.* I don't know why. I got little sleep last night."

Mark smirked. "The perils of being a parent."

"You got that right. Please remind me it's worth it?"

He chuckled. "Every bit of it. And having *kinner* sure teaches patience."

Judith smiled. "I don't know how you manage with your brood and helping me."

Mark's face clouded. "Sis, I actually need to speak to you in private before we have lunch."

She clasped her hands tighter together. "Is here alright?"

He glanced over his shoulder, noticing several families milling nearby, engaged in lively conversation. Mark pointed towards a nearby Cedar. "Let's talk there. In the shade."

Judith wondered why he looked so serious. She hoped all was fine at his home. *He would have said straightaway if Ruby or the children were ill.* Mark held her gaze for a few seconds before speaking. Her brother had the same colour hair as her: dark with chestnut highlights.

Beyond that, he was sturdier. He had a stocky build while she was more slender. They both had the apple cheeks of their mother and the determination of their father.

"Sorry, Judith but I am not coping with helping on your farm and running my business." He ran a hand through his bushy beard. "I'm exhausted. I have little energy for the *kinner* at the weekends. Ruby is concerned about the stress I'm under too. At her insistence, I went for a checkup at the doctor this week."

He paused. "Turns out my blood pressure is high. I refused medication but I agreed to make lifestyle changes starting with reducing the number of hours I am working."

"I've been worried about you too. I know you've made tremendous sacrifices helping me. *Danke* for all you're doing."

Mark took her hand and patted it. "I'm glad to have helped you. But I need to focus on my business and *familye* now. I can help you for one more month but that's all. You need to employ someone to work on the farm."

"I understand that you can't keep on working the long hours you've been putting in. I am very grateful you can help me another month. But I don't like the idea of hiring a manager."

His eyes were puzzled. "Why not? You would never cope handling the farm alone. Perhaps you should consider selling it. You could invest that money in a small business. Maybe get a job in a bakery."

"I would see even less of Isaiah than I do now."

"Wouldn't be forever. I'm sure you will remarry eventually."

Why was everyone suddenly set on her marrying again? Judith spoke firmly, "I am keeping the farm. That won't be changing."

"But things have to change," Mark said equally firmly.

"*Jah*," Judith mumbled.

Mark's eyes remained fixed on hers. His tone gentler, he said, "I have an old friend in mind to run your farm. From what I have gathered, he knows a lot about horticulture. And he is a reliable *mann*. He would work hard. I'm sure of that."

Judith rolled her shoulders, still stiff from wrapping elastic around multiple bunches of spinach. "Thanks for the suggestion but I would rather not bring in a manager."

Mark frowned in exasperation. "Mind telling me why not?

"He will probably want to alter the way we do things. I have kept the farm sustainable for over two years. I won't give up on it now."

"Wasn't saying you had to give up on it," Mark muttered. "Sometimes you are too stubborn for your own *gut*."

"I admit I have a stubborn streak. Let's get lunch if there's any left."

Mark's eyes softened. "You've had a rough time. Maybe you can reconsider in a month or so."

"Maybe." *She wasn't making any promises.*

CHAPTER 3

$\mathcal{I}$t was almost November, and Judith had managed the farm without Mark's help for a month. He checked on her every week and loaded produce on the wagon every Friday to save her from having to put her back into the heavy work by herself. Beyond that, Judith was handling everything. After she put Isaiah to bed at night, she worked several more hours, packing orders. When she eventually got to bed, it was often well past eleven.

The fresh produce continued to sell well but Judith was beginning to make mistakes with the paperwork. Something she had never done before. That week, she had apologized to a couple of clients for getting their orders muddled up. They forgave her after she told them she would sort out the problem the next day. Judith was exhausted from all she had to do.

Keeping tabs on everything was a nightmare. On Saturday morning, Isaiah kept on nagging her to take him to the play area conveniently placed in the middle of the farmer's market.

"Why not, *Mamm*?"

Losing patience at his continued nagging, Judith snapped. "Because I said *nee*, that's why. Stop asking. I'm not changing my mind."

"It's not fair," Isaiah said moodily. He pressed a finger on a tomato as if to annoy her. Judith ignored him as several customers approached her stall.

"I'll have three bunches of spinach, please," a woman said, while another waited her turn.

Finally done helping them, Judith glanced behind her to thank Isaiah for behaving. He was nowhere to be seen. She craned her neck, staring down the aisle in her section. There was no sight of her precious two-year-old. Just a steady queue of customers, all grown-ups.

Now she had done it! Besides herself with self-recrimination, her hands shaking, Judith placed the *Back Soon* sign on the table. She glanced towards a neighboring stallholder where Marie was popping more pies into her small oven, her bangles jangling.

"Excuse me, Marie," Judith asked in a strained voice. "Have you seen Isaiah?"

Marie shook her head remorsefully. "No, I haven't. Sorry, my dear." She crossed the passage to Judith's stand. "Haven't seen him in the last couple of minutes. Where did you see him last?"

Judith blushed, embarrassed to admit her shortcomings as a mother. "He was right here. I was helping customers. When I turned around, he was gone."

Marie peered at her, no judgment in her gaze. "I'll help you look for the tot. Sure he is close by."

"Thank you. That is kind. I will start at the playground." Judith stared at her with alarmed eyes.

Marie gave her a sympathetic smile. "I'm sure we'll find him. I'll check the stalls. Maybe he saw someone he recognized and wandered off to say hello."

Judith walked briskly towards the playground, which was out of sight. Her heart was beating as fast as if she had run a race. The playground came into view, with excited children of all ages taking turns on the climbing frames and the swings. Isaiah wasn't among them.

She marched to the bathrooms. Maybe he'd gone there first. A man glanced her way as she hovered outside the entrance to the men's cloakroom.

"Women's is on the other side of the building," he mumbled.

She nodded, staying where she was. "Thanks." He gave her another sweeping glance as he walked past her in the direction of the tent housing the stalls. Judith fastened the bow under her chin of her *Kapp*. She waited a few more minutes, feeling foolish as various men walked past in dribs and drabs, all glancing her way.

She sighed heavily, praying that Isaiah was safe when he failed to emerge from the building. Retracing her path to the playground with determined steps, she searched there again. *Still not there.* In a panic and close to tears, she pressed a trembling hand to her mouth. Judith hesitated, considering whether to ask the organizer of the farmer's market to announce a lost child. *Her child.*

"*Mamm!*" Isaiah's bright voice called as he exited the tent of stalls. Judith's face lit up in a delighted smile as he ran towards her, his hat on skew.

"There you are! Thank goodness!"

"I wasn't lost," Isaiah announced proudly as he hurtled against her dress. "Saw a friend."

She hugged him close, crying with relief. "I'm glad. I love you."

"Love you, too," he mumbled. He stared at her with big eyes. "Why are you crying?"

She dabbed her cheek with her sleeve. "I was scared I had lost you. SorrymI was so grumpy."

Isaiah hung his head. "Sorry I was naughty."

Marie reached them, beaming. "Found him, then he rushed off when he saw you." She sounded out of breath as if she had raced after him.

"Thank you for your help, Marie. May I treat you to a *kaffe*?"

"I was happy to help. A coffee would be marvelous. I take two sugars."

Isaiah peered at his mother, looking proud. "That's nice of you." Judith straightened his hat, smiling.

Marie patted Isaiah's shoulder."You have a nice Mama. You take good care of her."

Isaiah giggled. "She takes care of me."

"I better get back to my stall," Marie said. "There is probably a line of people already, hungry for pies."

"Please keep two for us," Judith called. Marie smiled, giving an answering wave.

"I like pies," Isaiah said, sticking close to his mother.

"So do I." Taking her son's hand, Judith acknowledged that she couldn't manage all alone.

She called at Mark's house the very next day, bringing Isaiah along. Judith was glad to see Mark's buggy parked out front. She felt bad for arriving unannounced on a Sunday morning, but she needed to speak to him urgently. Before things got completely out of hand.

Ruby opened the door, smiling broadly. "*Hallo*! This is a pleasant surprise."

"*Hallo*, Ruby." Her sister -in-law's greeting dissolved Judith's awkwardness at turning up without letting them know. Ruby wore an apron and had Charlie and Hannah at her side, their hands covered with flour.

"*Hallo*, Auntie Judith!" the children chorused. They peeked at Isaiah, giggling as they held up their floury hands.

Judith burst into laughter. "*Hallo*, there. Looks like you are baking."

Charlie's eyes were filled with mischief. "Uh-huh. We are making a cake. We were going to surprise you."

"Some surprise," Ruby said dryly, shaking her head at him. She waved Judith and Isaiah in. "Have a seat in the living room while I call Mark. He was planning on visiting you later. Saves us a trip."

Surprised to hear that, Judith smiled. "*Danke.* Sorry, I arrived unannounced. I need to ask Mark something important if he can spare a moment." She looked at Isaiah. "You stay here with me."

"Aw," he said, casting a longing look his cousin's way as they disappeared down the hall, towards the kitchen. Ruby paused in the doorway, staring at Judith.

"Isaiah can help the *kinner* cut the cookie dough if that's okay with you. We are also making cookies."

"That's fine," Judith said lightly. "He will enjoy that." Isaiah smiled and ran to join his cousins.

Ruby rolled her eyes in mock dismay. "I will supervise them. Make sure there isn't a flour fight."

"Just as well."

Ruby shook her head as if remembering the reason Judith had popped around. "I will call Mark. He shouldn't be long. He is pottering in the shed."

Mark strolled into the lounge, looking relaxed, his shirt sleeves rolled up. "Hey! *Gut* to see you."

"Hey!"

The siblings smiled at each other, giving each other the chance to speak.

"I came to ask something, Mark."

He grinned. "So Ruby told me. Ask away." He sat down, in no hurry.

"You were right. I need a manager for the farm. Is that friend of yours still available?"

Mark scratched his forehead. "I reckon he still is. The last time we spoke, he mentioned wanting to return to Lancaster. He has lots of horticulture experience, so managing a farm would be ideal."

Judith gave a relieved sigh, the tension leaving her shoulders. "That's *gut* to hear." She tilted her head. "He used to live here?"

"*Jah*. He left eight years ago when he was eighteen. Remember Samuel Fischer? He has been living with his aunt and uncle. They trained him in horticulture."

Judith looked at her brother, stunned. "The same Samuel Fischer I courted for a short while after I was baptized?"

"*Jah*, that's him."

She narrowed her eyes. "Was this his idea?"

Her brother smirked. "So what if it was? Samuel asked after you recently. Phoned me while I was at work. I told him you were struggling. He said he'd be happy to help out if that suited you."

Judith was struggling to believe this. *After all these years?*

"I can give him a call in the morning as it's a business requirement for your farm. There's nothing personal between you anymore. May I ask him if he's still interested?"

"Interested?" Judith sputtered, losing her cool. *Was this a good idea?*

Mark tapped the arm of his chair with his hand as if the deal was fair accompli. "Still interested in working for you. Managing the farm."

"*Jah*, you might as well. *Danke.*" *There was no other choice.* Their relationship was cut short when Samuel took up the offer of moving to his aunt and uncle to learn the business of horticulture. They had written to one another for a while but as he wasn't coming back, the courtship had ended.

It had been years since they had any contact. Then she had fallen in love with Isaac and married him. She had all but forgotten Samuel.

"Stay for lunch?"

"*Jah, danke*. That would be lovely."

Mark grinned. "Splendid! Now if you'll excuse me, I must finish fixing a gate at the back. Needs a new hinge."

She had to ask. "Did Samuel never marry?" If her brother thought her question strange, he didn't show it.

"*Nee*. He has never married."

"Are you matchmaking?" she asked. The twinkle in her brother's eyes bothered her.

He didn't give her a direct answer. "I think he would make a great farm manager. Further than that is up to you."

"He can stay in the *dawdihaus* if he needs accommodation. Not in the main *haus*."

Mark lifted a brow. "I will be sure to tell him. When would you like him to start?"

She managed to keep her nerves from showing. "The sooner the better. We can discuss salary when we meet. I have asked around, I know what the going rate is for a farm manager."

Mark stood up, studying her with amused eyes. "From what I have heard, Samuel is a better manager than most. You might have to negotiate."

"Won't be the first time," she mumbled.

"Just a word of advice," Mark said quietly. "Samuel isn't a shy teenager anymore. He's a *mann*."

Judith blinked. "I had figured that out already."

Mark laughed. "Then you'll agree that it would be best if *Mamm* popped around three times a week to keep an eye on Isaiah. We don't want folk speculating about the nature of your relationship with Samuel."

If she didn't know her brother better she would have thought he was pulling her leg. *Or was he?*

CHAPTER 4

Samuel didn't know what to expect when he met Judith again. He had wanted to move back to Lancaster several years ago. Getting back with Judith wasn't his motivation for suggesting he manage her farm. He was upset when he heard she was widowed, and not just because she had lost her husband. Raising a child on her own – her first – would be difficult. He couldn't imagine how disappointed she must have been not to be able to share the joy of having a son with her husband. How deep her grief must have been at losing Isaac. Mark told him that Judith's boy, Isaiah was two years old and a bright, sunny-natured child.

Sounded like Isaiah had inherited Judith's

sunny disposition. Samuel had always liked that about her. All those years ago, when he was eighteen, and he announced he had to leave Lancaster to learn horticulture with his uncle and aunt, Judith didn't complain. He had struggled at school as he had dyslexia. That made reading difficult.

His spelling was still atrocious. If a letter was important, Samuel got someone to check the spelling before sending it. He was confident these days but he had been bullied at school, called stupid and worse. It still hurt remembering the taunts of some of his classmates. Samuel shoved the memories aside.

He would always be grateful to his aunt and uncle for teaching him about horticulture and cultivation. They told him he had a rare gift for propagating plants. At first, he struggled to accept their words as true. Now he knew his thirst for knowledge and to understand why plants thrived under certain conditions and not under others was his gift to the world. He didn't feel useless anymore.

His enthusiasm to advance his skills was as strong as the first day he set foot in their nursery. Then, his prime reason for leaving Lancaster had been to escape the bullying. Now he knew better than to run away from difficult situations. His personality had changed. He was much stronger.

Wiser in the ways of the world too. Samuel knew his worth now. He wouldn't buckle under pressure, or accept second best for himself. If he had stuck to believing the cruel words directed at him, he would have been as bad an enemy to himself as those foolish bullies. Just settling for any old job would have been a cop-out.

Oddly, the bullying had taught him an important truth. While there were things he couldn't change, like unkind people, he could refuse to accept their labels and judgments. He was no better or worse than the next man. He was Samuel, the horticulturist. Finding his purpose had changed everything. Judith had always believed in him which was more than he could say for himself.

"There are many things you can become *gut* at," she said fiercely once. "Reading and writing isn't everything. You are very observant. *Gut* at arithmetic. Handsome too."

"You think I'm handsome?" he asked softly.

Judith blushed. "Uh-huh. But we shouldn't speak of such things."

Samuel still remembered how good he'd felt at her thinking he was handsome. Not out of vanity but out of wanting her to find him desirable. They only kissed a few times. A gentle, chaste kiss just before they reached her parents' farm. Only for a few stolen seconds. Then he would flick the reins so the horse and buggy moved forward again.

Those days seemed a lifetime ago. Samuel had no claim to Judith now and she was his employer. He would never step out of line. Samuel was happy at the thought of helping her, as a young widow and mother with too much responsibility to bear alone. She had helped him in her sweet way when he was a teenager and he was glad to be able to repay her kindness.

Keeping the farm said a lot about her determination. Judith had always been determined, even as a seventeen-year-old when he courted her. He chuckled, remembering how hesitant her father had been about him courting her. Judith was only seventeen then.

Ben Yoder shook his head. "I'm not sure that Judith is mature enough to marry in a few years. She seems more focused on having fun with her friends than starting a *familye* in the near future."

Samuel's quick answer saved the day. "Sir, I'm sure you are right. But I am keen on Judith. With your permission, if I don't ask her whether she would like to court me, another fellow may beat me to it."

Judith's father roared with laughter. "Well I never! Spoken like a *mann*. Thought you were just a skinny eighteen-year-old. *Jah*, you may court Judith, with my blessing."

"*Danke*, Sir."

Mr. Yoder chuckled, pointing a finger skywards. "Make sure you behave, young *mann*. Remember, I was your age once."

Samuel's thoughts returned to the present as he saw Judith's farm. He pushed his hat back to get a better look. Mark's directions were spot on and so it was easy enough to find. When they met for a cold drink earlier, his friend described the farm-house as being midway down a green rolling hill with cornfields dotted for miles to the west of it.

Mark had leaned close, grinning. "If you see a boy perched on a horse, that would be Isaiah."

"Riding so young?"

"*Nee*, his *grossmammi* leads the horse. Don't you worry? Starry Night is the most docile mare in Pennsylvania. She is retired from farm work. Gets spoiled with carrots all day long."

Samuel and Mark had always got on well, even as teenagers. As an adult, Samuel appreciated

Mark not bringing up the topic of having courted Judith once, although it was many years ago. It would have been awkward. While Samuel wasn't seeking to win back Judith's heart, he was looking forward to meeting her again. *Undeniably.*

Judith's offer for him to help out on the farm had been a welcome surprise. Samuel was trying to establish a propagation nursery but he had no land of his own. He had experimented at his uncle and aunt's nursery with considerable success but he had a bolder vision than a suburban nursery. He hoped to eventually supply farmers for miles around with fruit trees and other plants. He had plenty of ideas.

He needed more income to start his venture. Judith and he still had to discuss his salary and Samuel was sure she would be fair. Mark had mentioned that she had done her homework and that she knew the going rate for a farm manager. He would be fair too. He understood the farm had taken a small knock in profits in the two years since Isaiah was born.

Judith must have felt pulled in all directions. Samuel thought it was generous of Mark to help his sister out like he had. The Yoders had a strong family bond. Samuel, too. He was going to miss his aunt and uncle but he was excited about the chance to help out on Judith's farm. His parents had passed away when he was twenty in a boating accident.

That had been a huge shock and a wake-up call. He wanted to live his best life for his parents. Returning to Lancaster was like coming full circle for several reasons. Healing his past. Honoring his parents by becoming a man they would have been proud to call their son.

At least they had lived to see him gain confidence as he learned as much as he could about cultivation and propagation. That was some comfort. *Miss you both so much.*

Samuel was glad it was November and he wasn't arriving all sweaty. Some dust had settled on his trouser legs from when he got out to pick plants at the roadside a few miles back. He wanted to ask Judith what they were. They had berries on them. He doubted they were poisonous but he would make sure about that.

Especially with an inquisitive toddler about the place. He tucked the cuttings in his jacket pocket, to be on the safe side. He parked the buggy outside Judith's barn.

"He's here!" a boy yelled, turning his head

towards the farmhouse. He was stationed on a wagon near a chicken coop, sitting on the seat as if he were the driver.

"*Hallo*, Mister!" he shouted, clambering down and racing towards him. He reached him, his eyes bright with excitement. "Are you helping *Mamm*?"

"Hey! *Jah*, I am." Samuel climbed down from the buggy. He swept his hat off and got down on his haunches so their eyes were level.

The blue-eyed boy took his hat off. "Pleased to meet you," he mumbled, shyer now that they were face to face.

Samuel grinned. "Pleased to meet you. You can call me Samuel. Are you by any chance Isaiah?"

He gave an impish smile. "Yip."

"Thought so." Samuel straightened up, putting on his hat again. "Where's your *Mamm*?"

Isaiah's confidence returned, as he swivelled to stare at the house. "Inside. I'll take you."

"*Danke*. Hold on." Samuel leaned inside his buggy and took out a box. "Okay, I'm ready now."

Isaiah turned to him as they walked slowly towards the house. "She's fussing."

"I promise to behave." *Why in heaven's name did he say that?*

Isaiah chortled.

48

"Hey, Samuel," Judith said from the doorway in that clear voice he remembered so well.

She was even prettier. "Hey, Judith." He took off his hat, the box still under his arm.

Judith smiled, a hint of laughter in her green eyes. "Looks like you have your hands full. May I take that?"

"It's heavy," he protested, accidentally brushing her arm with the brim of his hat.

She tinkled with laughter. "I meant your hat."

"I'm managing fine, *danke*." The lost years shrank between them as he gazed at her, noticing a freckle under her eye that hadn't been there before. It added to her beauty.

Isaiah grinned at his mother. "We made friends." Judith blinked, giving Samuel a questioning look.

"I did introductions earlier," Samuel explained. He pointed his chin towards the box still under his arm. "Mind if I put this down?"

Her hand flew to her mouth. "Of course. Please *kumm* in. Welcome to our home."

Keen to get rid of the heavy weight, he walked ahead of her to the kitchen. He followed the smell of pastry and set the box carefully on the table and then smiled at Judith. Her cheeks flushed as she smiled back.

"That's better." Samuel rubbed his shoulder dramatically as he caught Isaiah peering at the box with interest.

"What's in there?" Isaiah asked.

"A raspberry bush for your mother."

"For me?" Judith laughed. "That wasn't necessary."

Samuel shrugged. "Needed a home."

Her eyes searched his as if recalling a conversation. Samuel remembered the sadness he'd felt after they decided not to continue writing to each other. He had been away three months and was sure he wanted to stay with his aunt and uncle for good. *Not anymore.*

Samuel pointed at the sealed lid of the box. "Got a knife?"

She nodded, opening a drawer and handing him one.

Isaiah tugged at his sleeve. "Why's it in a box?"

"Didn't want soil all over my buggy."

Isaiah grinned. Samuel slid the knife between the cellotape, tugged, and split the sticky line. He folded back the flap and lifted the raspberry bush for their inspection. Judith picked up Isaiah, placing him on her hip to have a better look.

"Still in good shape," Samuel remarked.

Judith giggled. "Looks healthy."

"Took *gut* care of her."

Judith stared at the plant. "Can you plant them at this time of year?"

"Sure you can. The roots develop stronger in the spring if you plant them in the winter."

"Thanks for bringing it. I don't have a raspberry bush."

Samuel returned the plant to the box. "I know. I asked Mark whether you had one."

She raised her brows. "Surprised he knew I didn't."

"To be honest, he wasn't certain. Then he said you would have offered him raspberry pie if you had."

"Smart conclusion." Her eyes darted to the oven. "Which reminds me!" She turned off the gas oven and then looked over her shoulder. "I made a meat pie. Would you like to join us for a light supper after I have taken you to the see the *dawdihaus*?"

"*Jah*, Ma'am. *Danke*!"

She laughed. "Please call me Judith. Calling me ma'am makes me feel like a schoolteacher."

Samuel cleared his throat. "I'd like to first plant the raspberry bush if you show me where you would like it to go. Needs a sunny spot." He smirked. "I'm sure you know that."

She nodded, distracted as Isaiah whispered in her ear. "You can plant it near the shed. Would be nice to screen that off. Create shade."

He leaned towards her with a conspirational expression. "It's a shrub, not a tree."

"*Jah*." She gave a self-conscious laugh, putting Isaiah down again. "You'll find a spade in the shed. It isn't locked."

"*Danke*, but I'll use the one I brought with me. It's the perfect size."

Judith threw her head back and laughed. "Spoken like a horticulturalist."

"Could Isaiah help me? *Kinner* like getting their hands dirty."

"*Jah*, he would like that."

Samuel grinned. "Helping me or getting his hands dirty?"

"Can I dig?" Isaiah asked, his eyes wistful.

"Sure you can. I need some more muscles."

Isaiah jumped on the spot. "Let's go!"

Judith touched his cheek. "Be careful. Don't get in Samuel's way."

Samuel's heart was touched by Isaiah's eagerness to help. Being a boy, he probably relished having a man around the place, although he saw a lot of his uncle by the sound of things. He might have to watch against Isaiah becoming too attached to him.

Judith called after them, "There's cold drink in the kitchen when you're finished."

Samuel paused in the passage to be sure she could hear him. "*Danke!*"

Later, over an early supper, Judith suggested that Samuel use a piece of her farmland to begin his nursery. "There is plenty of ground. I would like to help you get started."

"That would be fantastic. I will pay you for the water."

She frowned. "Please don't do that. We have plenty of water. We drilled a borehole last year. Mark got a *gut* deal through a contact of his."

"I'm impressed!"

"*Danke.* I reached a point where it was to get a borehole or give up farming. I would never have forgiven myself if I'd done that." Her eyes filled with sudden tears.

Samuel broke the silence. "You have coped admirably. And you are doing a brilliant job raising Isaiah. He is a wonderful child."

"*Danke.* I take it day by day. He likes having you around."

Samuel's eyes searched hers, remembering how she had teased him as a teen. Helped him to stop being bothered by not getting good marks for reading and writing.

"You're a head taller than your bullies," she once said. "And far nicer. Ever stop to think they might be jealous of you?"

Now as the winter days grew shorter, Samuel ignored the moments where there was a spark between them. *It was too soon to court her if she even wanted to.*

54

CHAPTER 5

*J*udith was thankful it was Spring. She laughed as Isaiah sprayed the raspberry bush with water from a water can. He turned to her, drips of water on his shirt.

"It's getting lots of leaves, *Mamm*."

"I see that! You are doing a great job taking care of it."

He plonked the watering can down, inspecting his pride and joy. "Will we get raspberries soon?"

"Only next year, in the summer. I asked Samuel."

Isaiah straightened up, his eyes forlorn. "Aw! I wanted them sooner."

Judith picked him up and kissed his cheek, thankful they could find such joy in simple acts like taking care of a raspberry bush. "*Gut* things *kumm* to those who wait."

He wrapped his arms around her neck. "I'd like berries now."

Judith ruffled his hair. "Me, too." She put him down. "Are you hungry?"

He nodded his head vigorously.

"We've got rolls and *wurst* for lunch."

"Yum!"

"Let's take Samuel lunch too. He is so busy he often skips lunch. He is planting lots of trees. He must be very hungry."

Isaiah nodded, smiling broadly. "I want to go."

Samuel's nursery was a fair walk from the farmhouse. Close to the dirt entrance road, it was sheltered by red maples. Samuel had chosen the location based on the rich soil quality and easy access to the road. They arrived to see him, lugging yet another tree into a large pot.

He had completed a whole row of trees already which must have taken some serious slog. He heard their footsteps and looked up, dusting the earth off his hands. His eyes lit up.

"Hey, there!"

"*Daed!*" Isaiah shouted, running towards him

with the exuberance of a toddler. "We brought lunch!"

Samuel froze on the spot. Then recovering his composure, he opened his arms wide. Isaiah clung to his trouser legs, smiling as if he'd won a prize at a fair.

"*Daed*," he crooned. Samuel's eyes widened as he exchanged a glance with Judith. She decided not to correct Isaiah, not wanting to spoil his joy.

"Sorry," Judith mouthed silently.

Isaiah held a finger over his mouth. He stared at the basket Judith held. "You brought me lunch?"

Happy to change the subject after Isaiah called him *daed*, Judith's words tumbled out. "*Jah*. Just a simple lunch of *wurst* and rolls. I thought you'd be hungry after putting in so much work." He bent to retrieve his hat from the gravel path, his face hidden from her.

"*Danke* very much." Then he stood up, his dark brown eyes meeting hers with a directness that took her breath away. "Are you joining me?"

"We're eating in the *haus*," she stammered.

"Aw!" Isaiah said plaintively.

"Better listen to your *Mamm*," Samuel said. He winked at him. "Maybe we can eat lunch together another day."

Judith stared at Samuel. *Why not?* She could do with the company.

"How about meeting here for lunch every weekday?" she asked, holding her breath. She hoped he wouldn't think her forward for suggesting that.

"That would be marvelous. Gets lonesome here sometimes, although I love the work." He shifted on his feet, keeping his gaze on her. "I'm happy to contribute towards the cost. Providing lunch wasn't part of our arrangement."

Judith frowned, perplexed at him paying when they had become friends as much as colleagues. "I'm happy to bear the cost. You have more than covered your keep, if you're concerned about that." She laughed. "Speaking of which, I did the books yesterday.

"Sales have picked up remarkably in the three months since you joined us. Beyond what I hoped."

His eyes brightened. "In that case I accept. *Danke.*"

She set the basket down. "Better eat your lunch while it's warm. There's homemade lemonade too."

"Feel like it's my birthday."

"How old are you?" Isaiah asked.

Samuel chuckled. "Twenty-six."

"So old?" Isaiah stared at Samuel like he was his hero.

Judith interrupted her son before he got a chance to embarrass her again. "No more questions, Mister. Let's go eat lunch."

Isaiah nodded solemnly, peering at Samuel. "Bye."

Samuel patted his back. "Bye. See you tomorrow!" He turned to Judith, holding her gaze again. "Looking forward to chatting tomorrow."

Aware of Isaiah's eyes on her, Judith said politely, "See you around twelve thirty."

Safer to think of him as her farm manager – nothing more than that.

Walking home, Judith considered how to explain to Isaiah why he couldn't call Samuel *daed.* "Isaiah, remember I told you your *daed* is in heaven?"

Isaiah threw the stone he was carrying, his face stubborn.

"I am sorry your *daed* went to heaven and you didn't know him."

"Doesn't matter," he mumbled.

"Wait a moment," Judith said softly. She took his hand, stopping in the shade of a tree so she could see his face clearly.

Isaiah's mouth formed an obstinate line. "Samuel's my *daed*," he grumbled, his blue eyes narrowing. Judith let go of his hand, staring into the distance. Praying she didn't make a hash of explaining where Samuel fitted in the scheme of things.

"Samuel is our friend," she said finally. "We care about him. But he isn't your father."

Isaiah scraped his boot in the dirt, making a snaky shape. "*Daed*," he muttered, fixing his gaze on the ground.

Judith gave a mighty sigh. She decided to stop her explanations for the time being. Isaiah was only two and a half. She couldn't help it that he wanted a father. *Needed one.* She decided it would be better to discuss the matter with Samuel. She couldn't allow Isaiah to call Samuel *daed*.

"Race you to the *haus*," Judith said.

Always up for a dare, Isaiah's chin lifted. "On your marks."

She nodded, drawing a line with the tip of her shoe. "There's the starting line for you. I will make one further back for me because I'm taller."

Isaiah snorted, turning around to watch her as she made another line. "Easy peasy," he retorted, clapping his hands. Judith stifled a laugh as Isaiah shuffled his feet in the earth, becoming impatient. She hitched her dress up slightly, knotting the bottom so she wouldn't trip.

She called, "Only run when I say go!"

He rolled his eyes. "*Jah!*"

"Ready, get set...Go!" They set off. Her son ran as fast as he could, laughing. She ran slowly, deliberately drawing level with him and not going any faster. After several moments of running, Judith clutched her side dramatically.

"I have a stitch."

He peered over his shoulder. "C'mon. Not far!"

"I'm trying!" she called, letting him get well ahead of her. Judith giggled as her son reached the house. Isaiah jumped in the air when he reached the front door.

"Winner takes all!"

"You beat me fair and square," she said, out of breath. "Well done."

"You ran fine," he said, giving a smug smile.

"I better practice if I want to beat you next time," she said thoughtfully.

"I'm hungry," he said, tugging at her dress.

"Sit down and I'll dish up lunch."

He sat down, suddenly as good as gold. "*Danke, Mamm.*"

As agreed, they settled into a routine of taking lunch to Samuel on weekdays. Judith enjoyed the change in scenery. Samuel cut some logs to provide stumps to sit on. Isaiah didn't mind that his feet didn't touch the ground as long as he got a chance to chat with Samuel. Samuel sorted out the *daed* issue the very first time they ate lunch together in the nursery.

He leaned towards Isaiah, his dark eyes earnest. "Isaiah, I meant to tell you this yesterday. You and your *mamm* are my best friends. I'm happy about that."

Judith blushed, glad Samuel wasn't looking her way. Isaiah beamed at his mom, then he took a hearty bite of his chicken sandwich. Samuel caught Judith's eye. She gave him a warm smile, then glanced at her lap. When he looked at her silently with soft eyes, she would imagine what it would be like to be kissed by him.

Did he ever think that too?

Samuel turned to Isaiah. "I am not your *daed*," he said gently. "But I care about you very much. Your mother, too."

Isaiah nodded, lifting his face so the sun hit his chin. "Friends."

Judith was astounded that Isaiah accepted

Samuel's explanation so readily. Maybe it was the way he said it, rather than what he said. *What did Samuel mean when he said he cared about her?*

"I am happy to be part of your little *familye*," Samuel said. He grinned at Judith. "Very happy."

Judith took a sip of her cold drink, trying not to read any more into what he said beyond friendship. It was true. Samuel had established himself as an integral part of their little family. It was so much nicer having him around. She wasn't lonely anymore.

But, rather than just appreciating Samuel's company after she had spent the better part of her days alone with Isaiah, she knew her feelings were deepening for the man she had once courted. They didn't always eat lunch together as both she and Samuel were occupied with planting, feeding, and watering plants. At month end, Judith needed to concentrate on the accounts for several days, intent on checking her sales thoroughly.

In May, six months after Samuel's arrival to help at the farm, Judith's mother, Sadie asked the question that had been bothering Judith for several weeks.

"Are you and Samuel courting?"

Isaiah was out of earshot, thankfully. Her

mother had chosen to ask her while he was having his afternoon nap. Judith shook her head.

"We are just friends. That's all. It's *gut* to see Samuel after all these years."

Her mother gave her a dismissive look. "Are you sure about that? Samuel and you look so comfortable together."

Comfortable?

Suddenly aware of deep disappointment, Judith paused to collect her thoughts. When Isaac died, her suffering was so severe that she feared she would never be able to love again. When Isaiah was born a month premature, loving her child eased some of her heartache. Now, miraculously, she was sure she could love again. Remarry. Maybe even have another child.

"You looked so sad then," her mother said quietly. "Is there something you need to talk about?"

Judith sighed. "*Danke, Mamm.* I am doing much better these days. But Samuel and I aren't courting. He has never asked me about courting. We have never gone on an outing together. You must have noticed that he always goes to church services alone. In his buggy."

Her mother shook her head. "I think Samuel

cares for you more than friendship. He probably travels alone out of consideration for you. What people might say." She sniffed. "Crying shame he hasn't asked you courting. I'm sure he has developed feelings for you. A virtuous woman like you. You should ask him what his intentions are."

Judith stared at her mother with shocked eyes. "*Mamm*. Samuel came here to help out on the farm. I could never ask him that! What would he think of me!"

Sadie pursed her mouth before she spoke again. "Suit yourself then. What's the alternative?"

"What do you mean?"

Her mother's eyes softened. "You aren't against the idea of courting him. So you have feelings for him. Do you want to still be dithering with friendship a year from now? Isaiah needs a father."

Judith drew in a sharp breath. "That's a bit harsh. It is up to Samuel to ask me courting."

Sadie clicked her tongue. "I just think you might need to encourage him. I know you're a *gut* girl. But you can let Samuel know you have feelings for him."

"I couldn't do that. What if he just wants to be friends?"

"Then you will know where you stand with

each other." Her mother gave her a tight smile. "You are just like your father. Won't be budged. Don't let that work against you."

Judith laughed. "Funny. I was thinking the same thing about you, *Mamm*, Please let things be."

"That's exactly what you shouldn't be doing," her mother said darkly. "But you're a grown woman. I won't speak of this again."

That will be the day.

"Nana!" Isaiah called, his hair all mussed up from his sleep as he tried to clamber on her lap.

"Hey, mischief!" Sadie kissed his cheek, beaming at him.

"You were cross," Isaiah said, staring at his mother.

"Not anymore." Judith got up and kissed the top of his head. Then surprising her mother, she kissed her cheek.

"What was that for?" her mother asked, giving her an indulgent smile.

Judith's eyes watered. "Just letting you know I love you, *Mamm*."

"I love you, too."

That evening, Judith invited Samuel to join her and Isaiah for dinner. They ate dinner together regularly. After she had tucked Isaiah in bed, she settled into a chair near the still-open window of the living room. Judith stretched her arms above her head before folding her hands neatly in her lap again.

"I love summer."

Samuel drew his chair closer, smiling. "Enjoy the long days?"

"*Jah*. And not having to shovel snow off the path or bundle up in loads of layers."

"Lots to enjoy about winter too."

Judith laughed. "You must think me boring, talking about the weather."

Samuel gave a hearty laugh, touching her hand lightly, before drawing back again, his eyes more reserved. "*You* are far from boring." He frowned, glancing at a clock on the wall. "It's getting late. I better go."

Remembering her mother's words that she needed to encourage him, Judith asked, "Going to church on Sunday?"

"I might not be able to go this Sunday. Need to sort something out."

"I will miss you," she said softly.

He smiled. "*Danke*. I might be out of town for the weekend. I was going to speak to you about it tomorrow. Would that be alright? I promise to be back Sunday evening."

He hadn't said he'd miss her. They were just friends.

Judith gave him a too-bright smile. "Of course, you may go out of town. It's only one night you're away. I will manage." This time her disappointment was worse than when she was seventeen. He left then to sort out his life and he still had feelings for her. Now, he saw her just as a friend. A widow. A mother. Not as a potential wife.

"You sure you will be fine?" he asked, standing up and gazing at her with concern.

She rose from her chair. "*Jah*, I might go into town on Saturday. Meet a friend."

He nodded as if his mind was elsewhere. "That's settled then. *Danke* for a lovely evening."

"Anytime." *If only he had asked her.*

CHAPTER 6

*S*amuel had thought about his situation for weeks on end. Tossed and turned at night. Deliberated on what the sensible choice was. Another thing he had learned after leaving Lancaster all those years ago was never to make a hasty decision. His parents had made sure he understood that there would be long-term consequences for his decision to stay with his aunt and uncle. He gained knowledge as a horticulturalist. But he had paid the price too.

He and Judith had parted ways. She had married Isaac. Now the girl he had once courted was much older. Samuel had to decide what was best for him now. He couldn't go on like this. He wanted more from life. He was turning twenty-seven this year.

Most Amish men his age had been married several years already. His uncle had sent him a letter in May expressing concern about him living the life of a bachelor. That had prompted Samuel's decision to visit them that weekend a few months back. He first made a quick call to check if he could visit. They had a landline to allow them to receive business orders for their nursery.

"Misty Hills Nursery," Aunt Martha's energetic voice greeted. "Good morning."

"Good morning, Aunt Martha."

"Samuel! Ach, it is *gut* to hear from you." She paused briefly. "Is everything fine there?"

"*Jah*, I love it here. My job. The farm. Everything!"

"I am glad to hear that. You deserve the best. And Judith and her boy? How are they keeping?"

Samuel laughed. "Judith is more relaxed than when I arrived. The farm is showing a healthy profit. Isaiah has taken a shine to me. I'd like to ask your advice about that."

"We must talk soon. I must go. I need to attend to a customer."

"I understand. May I possibly visit this weekend?"

"Of course. When will you arrive?"

"Saturday, late morning."

"See you then! Bye."

"Bye."

That weekend, his aunt and uncle had told him he should follow his heart. Samuel hadn't done that yet. Judith sent him mixed signals. They were friends. There was no doubt about that. But he understood that Isaiah was her priority. It had only been two and a half years since she lost her husband. Judith might even harbor anger towards him for leaving, although that seemed unlikely. They had agreed to part ways.

But as a friend in Misty Hills had pointed out to him, sometimes people accept what they don't want. That might explain why Judith got shy whenever he touched her hand. Samuel made sure it was the lightest touch and brief. Judith would go quiet and her reaction confused him.

Judith had mentioned being tired that week. "Maybe I need a day off."

"That would do you *gut*," Samuel remarked. "I can cover for you if you need something attended to."

She smiled. "*Danke*. While the idea is very appealing, I don't know whether I should."

Samuel stopped shoveling earth into a wheel-barrow. He glanced her way as she sat on a tree stump near the shaded entrance to his nursery.

"What's stopping you?"

Judith shrugged. "Won't get much of a break anyway, looking after Isaiah. He is quite a handful at the moment. Yesterday he climbed up a stepladder in the barn, trying to reach the loft. *Gut* thing he didn't fall." Her forehead creased in worry. "I reached him in the nick of time."

"I'm sure your parents wouldn't mind taking care of him. You should take a day off. When was the last time you had a day all to yourself?"

She laughed. "Feels like never! Maybe I should ask my parents."

"I'm glad."

"*Danke*. Isaiah would love to see them. He hasn't seen his *grosspappi* since church a couple of weeks ago."

Now on her day off, Judith was bringing Samuel lunch as usual. He had never eaten a meal with her without Isaiah being there. Isaiah was an adorable, well-behaved boy but Samuel was looking forward to having Judith's undivided attention for a change. He hoped she would stay and chat for longer than usual. Samuel had deliberately started his workday much earlier so the bulk of the work was behind him.

He could always make up any lost hours on Saturday. Working in the nursery was an investment in his future. Even his latest project, adding an extra section of wooden poles for roofing, was worth the effort. He continued measuring and marking the distance in the ground, wanting to make good use of his time before she arrived.

"Hey, there! Maybe you should also take a day off?" Judith's voice rang out.

Samuel pocketed the measuring tape. "You reckon?"

Her green eyes sparkled. "Take it from me. A rest will do you *gut*."

"Could you stay longer today? Talk a while?" He grinned. "I started earlier, so I'm not slacking."

"Perhaps I should," she said softly. Their eyes held, their mutual attraction obvious.

That did it. "I've got something important to ask you," Samuel said, taking her hand.

She blinked, smiling. "What is that?"

Encouraged, he got down on one knee, smiling

tenderly. "Judith, would you do me the honor of marrying me?"

She stared at him disbelievingly and dropped his hand, bursting into tears.

The color drained from his face. Samuel stood, touching her arm gently. "Why are you so upset?"

Judith shook her head wildly and ran off, sobbing. Samuel stared after her in confusion, baffled by her reaction to his proposal. He stood in stunned silence, all hope of marrying the woman of his dreams fading. He walked to the spot where he had hoped to speak with her of a future together. According to his perspective, things between him and Judith had been progressing perfectly.

Samuel was in love with her and he doted on her little boy. How could he have misread her feelings for him? Dazed, he pressed his hands to his forehead, trying to make sense of what just happened. There had to be a reason she had reacted so strangely. If she was still traumatized at losing Isaac, he could make sense of that.

She acted as if she was desperate to get away from him. *If only she had explained.* He decided to deal with the facts at hand, to understand Judith's outburst. He picked up a twig, then threw it down, frustrated at his lack of understanding. He knew for sure that her little boy loved him. Samuel wasn't trying to manipulate his way into Judith's heart through her son.

He frowned in dismay. He thought Judith loved him as much as he loved her until the moment he proposed and she took off in apparent shock. He was at a loss for what to do. Should he finish his work on the farm and hope that she returned without seeking her out?

After she calmed down, maybe she would want to speak to him. That seemed unlikely when he recalled her frenzied sobbing. Maybe his wisest move would be to leave for his parents' home and wait to hear from her. He could leave a note, explaining that he would be back on Monday morning. That seemed like running away from the problem, something he vowed never to do in the future.

Or he could stay put, put in a few more hours of work, and get an early night. Samuel stared at the posts lying on the ground that he still had to install. He couldn't work that afternoon. He was too wound up to be able to concentrate.

Should he just pretend none of this happened? Carry on as before in the friend zone, working on the farm? That alternative would never work. There were her boy's feelings to think of too. He didn't want to disappoint Isaiah who might assume he would be around forever. Samuel couldn't become too attached to him either.

Samuel couldn't go on as before with Judith. He had revealed his feelings. Been rejected. The thought of her doing that had never occurred to him. He thought after all these months of being friends, she had developed feelings for him. Why else had she had him around for supper so often?

Why was she so upset?

All the questions in his mind were bringing him no closer to the answers. Judith was having a day off today and now she was so stressed, she wouldn't even speak to him. He clenched his jaw, wishing he could have that moment with her again. Maybe if he had approached her more gently. First told her he loved her. He should have waited for her reaction to his declaration before rushing in with an offer to marry her.

Probably wouldn't have altered anything.

Fed up with his gloomy thoughts, Samuel shifted his gaze. He ignored the basket Judith had left for him. He picked up a wooden post, wedging it under his arm like a rifle. He might as well finish extending the nursery as he planned. Sitting around feeling sorry for himself wasn't going to accomplish anything except make him feel worse.

He grunted as he placed the heavy post on the ground. He could cast cement around the base that afternoon and leave to see his aunt and uncle the next morning. *How would that help?* He pushed the log aside so it rolled away from him, feeling wretched.

Darn it! Why not eat the lunch Judith had brought him? No point in letting food go to waste. He lifted the material covering and lifted out a plastic container. He chucked it straight back again and stormed over to a tap attached to a hosepipe. He turned the water on, watering some newly planted fruit trees. The water trickling down their leaves reminded him of Judith's tears.

He returned to the tap, turning it off. He would rake up the leaves outside of his nursery and add them to the pile of grass cuttings to make mulch for his plants. He picked up a steel rake, dragging it across the ground in spurts of energy. Smudge, the stray cat that he had befriended shortly after arriving on the farm stared at him with wary eyes and then slunk off.

Even the cat couldn't stand his company.

"Hey, there!" Mark called from the road, seated in his idle buggy.

"Hey, Mark." Samuel waved him in, not able to smile. "Want a cold drink?" At least he could extend hospitality to his friend.

"Thank you. I could do with some."

Samuel ran his hand through his hair, remembering he'd left his hat at the tap. Didn't matter. Was well past noon already. Mark stepped down from the buggy, staring at him before tethering his horse to a hitching post. He sauntered towards him, his cheerful mood at odds with Samuel's frantic state of mind.

Samuel wasn't one for pretending everything was dandy when it wasn't. But he would do his best to be welcoming. He poured the lemonade Judith had brought into a plastic cup.

He extended an arm towards Mark. "Here you go."

Mark gave him a curious glance before taking the cup. "I was coming to visit Judith as she has the day off. Have you seen her?"

"She left about a half an hour ago. Should be at the *haus*." Samuel stared at the basket she had left, thinking of the panic he'd seen in her eyes before she ran off.

Mark took a sip of lemonade. "This tastes *gut*! Judith's?"

"Uh-huh." Samuel lifted his head to meet his concerned eyes. "Maybe I should have some." He took the flask out again, pouring himself a cup." He drained half the cold drink, then set it down on a small table he used to write notes on.

Mark stepped forward, his eyes crinkled against the glare of the sun. "You okay? You seem upset."

Samuel lifted his head. "I'm confused by something that happened earlier."

"Does this have anything to do with my *schweschder*?"

"How did you know??"

"She told me how you eat lunch together on most days. It's kind of obvious you're upset."

"Didn't mean to be rude," Samuel mumbled. "I'm sorry."'

"No offence taken. Want to talk about it?"

"I feel like an idiot."

Mark held up a hand. "Stop that talk. That's a lie if you believe that."

Samuel shrugged. "Maybe."

"Argue?"

Samuel frowned. "*Nee*. But I am baffled by your

schweschder's behavior."

Mark tilted his head. "That doesn't sound like Judith. She's easy to read."

"I agree. She is, usually."

"Tell me what happened. I wouldn't want some misunderstanding to mess up your friendship."

"Maybe you have gathered as much, but I care deeply for your *schweschder*."

Mark smiled, in no hurry to push him for details. "*Jah*, I thought as much. You would make a great couple."

"That's what I thought. When she brought lunch earlier, well..." He paused. "'I asked her to marry me. She burst into tears and ran off. Never gave a reason. I ate dinner with her and Isaiah last night. Everything was fine. I thought she had feelings for me too."

"You need to speak to her. Sort it out today. I'll go with you if you like, then leave you two alone. I am sure she cares about you very much. Judith has been much happier since you arrived. No doubt about that."

"Before we go find her, I'd like to put some concerns to you, if that's okay."

"I'm listening."

"Do you think she is angry with me for leaving

all those years ago?"

"Not at all. She told me she is proud of what you have learned. She speaks highly of you."

"At least I can scratch that concern off the list. Do you think it is too soon for Judith to consider marrying again? I understand her grieving Isaac. She loved him. Perhaps she isn't open to loving another *mann*."

Mark sighed. "*Jah*, she must miss Isaac. But I am sure she is open to falling in love again. Otherwise, why would she invite you to dinner? Maybe she is just scared of getting hurt again. Judith would be open to love again. For her sake and Isaiah's."

Samuel drained the remains of his cold drink. "*Danke*. That gives me hope. I'd like to talk to her now then."

"Hang on a minute, Samuel," Mark said firmly. "Let's say a prayer first."

Samuel nodded, bowing his head, and closing his eyes. He opened them afterward to see Mark smiling at him.

"As I said, I'm sure Judith cares about you."

"Hope you're right."

"Catch a ride with me. Let's get this sorted."

"Amen to that." Samuel showed the glimmer of a smile.

CHAPTER 7

Samuel climbed into Mark's buggy, noticing he had installed a new heater. Must have got it in preparation for winter. He remembered joking with him in January as they shared a ride, their teeth chattering. Even with the snow thawing around them, the cold wind had been bone-chilling. Now September, winter would be with them before they know it.

Mark turned to him. "I doubt Judith's gone straight home if she's upset."

Samuel's eyes brightened. "Where are you thinking she's gone?" Mark chuckled. "Her favorite spot by the stream. She likes to take Isaiah there too. She says it's peaceful."

"Any fish to be had there?"

"Some. Never seen any decent-sized ones." Mark laughed. "But I'm not much of a fisherman. Sure Judith wouldn't mind if you tried to catch a couple."

Samuel stared at him. "One thing at a time. Fishing is not my priority right now."

Mark smirked. "Unless we are talking about catching my *schweschder*."

"True," Samuel mumbled.

Mark peered at him before directing his gaze back on the stony farm track. "Don't worry. I am sure my *schweschder* isn't upset with anything you've done. The past couple of years have probably just caught up with her. She said she was tired."

"*Danke*. I sure hope you're right."

They traveled in silence until Judith came into view. She was sitting on the bank of the stream with her knees drawn up to her chin, staring at the water. Samuel's heart jumped. She looked so pretty, the dappled sunlight falling on either side of her, her silhouette the picture of femininity.

Mark chuckled. "What did I tell you?"

"You still think it's a *gut* idea to talk to her now?"

"Looks like the most romantic setting in the

world," Mark drawled. "Let's meet for a *kaffe* in the morning at Murphy's Coffee Shop and you can fill me in."

"Sounds good. Meet at eleven?"

"Perfect. *Danke* again."

Mark smiled, drawing his buggy to a standstill. "Hey, Sis!"

"Hey!" Judith waved at them. She stood, brushing down her dress. There was no hint of tears in her expression.

Mark smiled. "Would you like me to fetch Isaiah and bring him home later? I will leave you two to talk."

Judith nodded. "That will be marvelous. *Danke*." Her eyes moved to Samuel. "I'd like to talk."

Samuel nodded. "I'd like that too."

"I'll be off then," Mark said.

Samuel stepped down. "*Danke* for the lift and travel safe."

Mark grinned. "*Gut* luck," he mumbled. "See you later, Judith!"

Judith waved again. "*Danke!*"

As he walked towards her, Samuel prayed that he could accept whatever she had to tell him. She seemed entirely different from the person who had bolted earlier. She was relaxed.

Samuel smiled as he approached her. "Let's sit down. You looked so peaceful sitting here just now. Mark told me this is your favorite spot."

She laughed, sitting down again, her legs stretched out in front of her this time. "*Jah*, It's one of my favorite places on the farm. I must show you the other places."

"Judith, I'm sorry I upset you earlier. Do you mind telling me what was bothering you?"

"*Danke*, but I'm the one who needs to apologize. Not you."

Samuel nodded, pretending he was calmer than he felt. He didn't move closer or touch her hand. She was his closest friend. If she didn't love him, then he would have to accept that with good grace, even if that meant leaving her.

Judith smiled broadly. "I have had time to think about your proposal."

Samuel's heart beat wildly at her words.

"I would love to marry you," Judith said softly. "I love you too."

Samuel took her hand, his voice shaking with emotion. "I thought I had lost you again. Judith, *danke*. I love you so much and Isaiah too."

Her face was radiant. "You are so *gut* to both of us. I still need to explain why I burst into tears."

Samuel nodded, squeezing her hand. "Please tell me."

Judith dropped her gaze, looking towards the stream as if gathering her thoughts. Finally, she turned to gaze at him. "Marrying you, I felt as if I would be acting against my commitment to Isaac by contemplating a life for myself and Isaiah without him. I felt confused after I left you. It was wrong to rush off like that. I panicked."

That made sense. "*Danke* for your honesty, Judith. If you ever feel like that again for some reason please rather tell me so we can sort it out. I only want the best for you. Isaiah, too. We are going to be *familye* now."

"I am excited!"

He grinned. "Me, too. Now please tell me what changed your mind. Was it my *gut* looks or my winning personality?"

Judith giggled. "Both those reasons." Her eyes grew serious. "When I arrived here just now, I felt a huge sense of loss after not giving you an answer. That troubled me. Not just because I had disappointed you, but because I wanted to marry you. I decided to pray to *Gott* for guidance. And His answer was very clear."

Samuel peered at her. "Tell me more."

Her face glowed with happiness. "I heard *Gott* telling me *Samuel loves you. He can be your familye.*"

"That is incredible!"

"I heard those words," she whispered, still incredulous.

"I believe you." Samuel grinned. "I must remember to thank *Gott* for answering my prayer. Mark and I prayed before we came to find you."

Judith's eyes sparkled. "Have you eaten lunch? I see you took the basket out of the buggy."

Samuel smirked. "And I thought this was such a romantic moment. *Nee*, I haven't had lunch."

"This is a romantic spot for a picnic."

Samuel burst into laughter. "Let's eat something then." He opened the lid of the plastic container and held the container near her.

Judith took a sandwich. "Nothing like being happy to restore your appetite."

"I couldn't eat a thing earlier. *Gut* thing Mark came along when he did. He gave me hope."

"I'm sorry I gave you a fright."

"That's over now. I understand your actions now."

Judith nodded, her eyes soft. "When did you decide you wanted to marry me?"

Samuel gave an awkward laugh. "The very first week I arrived at the farm. That first Friday you brought me lunch and you and Isaiah joined me." He laughed. "Took me by surprise. There I was, a bachelor, my mind set on being a model farm manager and I was wondering what it would be like to kiss you."

She blushed. "You were pleased I brought you lunch?"

"Of course! That meant you liked me. Actions speak louder than words in my book." *Her sudden shyness was cute.*

Judith giggled. "It is just as well I brought you lunch. I felt awkward the first time I brought you your lunch."

He peered at her. "You didn't show it."

"As I recall, Isaiah did most of the talking."

Samuel roared with laughter. "True. And he called me *daed* a month later."

"That had me worried."

"Me, too. Just as well we are becoming a *familye*." They finished their lunch, content to sit in silence, enjoying each other's company and the peaceful setting.

Judith broke the silence. "Want some lemonade?"

Samuel pulled a face. "Confession time. There's only a drop left. Mark and I polished it off earlier."

"That will teach me. Rushing off like that."

Samuel poured her the rest of the cold drink. "For you."

"*Danke.*" She drank thirstily, then handed him the cup. "Have the last sip."

"Won't say no, *danke.*" Samuel packed their stuff back in the picnic basket. "Is there anything else that we need to talk about before Isaiah gets back?"

Judith looked pensive. "*Jah.* Could Isaiah call you *daed* now that we're engaged?"

He was sure of his answer. "*Jah*, he can call me *daed*. I'd like that."

Judith surprised him by resting her head on his shoulder. "*Danke!*"

Samuel drew an arm around her shoulder. He bent his head and kissed her briefly on the mouth. His head spun like it had when he was a teenager.

He took her hand. "I never asked you courting the second time."

Judith laughed. "You better ask my *daed* for my hand in marriage this weekend. I am sure he will approve. My parents already told me – several times – what a great couple we would make. I was never sure what I was supposed to do about that."

Samuel grinned. "Your *bruder* told me the same thing. By the way, I'm meeting Mark for *kaffe* tomorrow morning. Why don't you and Isaiah join us?"

"Hmm. *Danke* for the invitation but I think we should tell my parents first."

"*Gut* point."

They stared at each other, smiling.

Samuel gazed at her. "Any ideas, *liebe*?"

"I like you calling me *liebe*," she murmured. "When Mark brings Isaiah, could you cancel your *kaffe* date? So we can see my parents instead tomorrow?"

Samuel looked at her intently. "I have a better idea. Let's invite your parents to join us when we see Mark. You can ask your *schweschder* to join us."

Judith's eyes widened. "That's going to spring a surprise on them all. I'm not sure that's going to work. May might already have plans. She sees friends most Saturday mornings.

"Let's keep your original arrangement as it was. I can invite my parents and May for lunch on Sunday. We can tell them then."

"Sure we can do that. Agreed!"

Judith laughed. "I'm just wondering how you

and I are going to keep from blurting out our engagement to Mark."

"And don't forget Isaiah!"

They started laughing. Soon tears of laughter were streaming down their faces. Perhaps it was the relief of knowing they loved each other and were loved in return. Or maybe it was the sheer joy of being alive. Later, as Samuel repaired a window latch at the farmhouse, and Judith sat on the porch, they saw Mark approaching in his buggy, an excited Isaiah waving at them.

Judith walked to Samuel, laughing. "I've changed my mind. Could we tell Mark and Isaiah now? Our engagement is such happy news."

Samuel smiled. "I agree. It is happy news. It would be a shame not to share it with them. But I suggest I take you and Isaiah to your parents' *haus* immediately afterward to tell them and your *schweschder*. That seems the right thing to do."

He stood next to her, amazed at how his life had changed for the better. Samuel had made plenty of friends after he moved away from the town in which he had grown up but he had never met a woman he liked as much as Judith. He had courted another woman, Maria, for a year when he was twenty-one. He eventually called their courtship off when he realized that he still had feelings for Judith. It wouldn't have been right to marry Maria under a false pretext.

When he made discreet inquiries about how Judith was doing, it was too late to restore himself to Judith's affection. He learned that she was already engaged to Isaac. Samuel simply had to move on with his life and stop hankering for what might have been between the childhood sweethearts. Samuel threw himself into his work and told no one of his heartache. After a year, the severe disappointment faded at the lost opportunity to marry Judith.

"Hey!" Mark called, peering at them with interest as he strolled towards them. "I gather you enjoyed your afternoon."

Judith blushed. "Uh-huh." She glanced at Samuel. "You tell them."

Samuel smiled, putting an arm around her shoulder as if to steady her excitement. "Let's first see what Isaiah has to tell us."

Isaiah raced towards them, his hair disheveled, which was nothing unusual. "*Grossmammi* and *grosspappi* are on their way over here later!"

"Do they want to spend more time with you?" Judith asked playfully. She glanced at her brother.

"Sounds like you could have saved yourself a trip. I don't understand why they didn't rather bring Isaiah home later."

Mark smirked. "Seems like they have something to discuss with you and Samuel." He glanced at his watch. They should be leaving home just about now."

"What's going on?" Judith asked. She peered at her brother. "Is this your doing? Did you mention that Samuel had proposed?"

Mark nodded. "It kind of popped out."

"What popped out?" Isaiah asked, peering at his uncle.

Mark stared at him, saying nothing. "Hold on a moment, Isaiah." He turned to his sister. "*Daed* asked me whether you and Samuel were spending the day together."

"I told him you'd brought Samuel lunch but you didn't seem yourself."

"Just the thing to say to *Daed*," Judith mumbled.

"He pressed me for information. I'm sorry. It just came out that Samuel had proposed."

Mark turned to Samuel. "If you don't mind me saying so, you both looked very happy until I admitted my blunder. Have you made up?"

Samuel took Judith's hand. "May I tell Mark now?"

She giggled, gazing at her fiancé. "Please do. My entire *familye* is arriving here soon anyway."

"Judith and I are engaged."

Mark grinned. "Congratulations! That is amazing!" He patted Samuel's back. "Welcome to the *familye*." Then he kissed his sister's cheek. "I am very glad you're marrying Samuel."

Isaiah tugged on his mother's sleeve, wide-eyed. "Is Samuel going to be my *daed*?" he asked in a voice filled with longing.

Judith lifted Isaiah, kissing his cheek. "*Jah*, Samuel is going to be your *daed*."

Isaiah stared at Samuel in wonder. "*Daed*!"

The grown-ups laughed while Isaiah smiled as if he had just received the best news ever.

CHAPTER 8

*B*en and Sadie Yoder beamed at Judith and Samuel after they shared the news of their engagement later that evening as the families sat in Judith's living room. Mark left as soon as they arrived, not wanting his sister to be overwhelmed with receiving so many well-wishers at once. It was true. Judith was still amazed at becoming engaged. Having another opportunity at love.

Samuel took all the attention in his stride. He was a great help in making everyone welcome. He was busy, pouring cold drinks for everyone. Judith's parents and her younger sister, May, were clamoring for more details.

"I am so happy for you both!" May exclaimed.

Judith laughed. "I am as surprised as you are!" Samuel entered the living room, carrying a tray with their cold drinks.

"*Daed*," Isaiah said proudly. Judith smiled at her son. She had little hope of him going to bed early that evening. He could barely sit still, he was so excited.

"Isaiah, you must have a bath soon," she reminded him.

He pouted. "No bath."

Samuel jumped to Judith's assistance. "Isaiah, we are going out together as a *familye* tomorrow morning. Please do as your *mamm* says. You can stay up a little longer, then you must have a bath."

"Okay, *Daed*," Isaiah said, satisfied with that arrangement.

"Can I be one of your helpers at the wedding?" May asked Judith with an imploring expression.

"Of course," Judith said, hugging her. "You must also get a new dress." She rolled her eyes. "Not the same color as mine though!"

Sadie Yoder gazed at her daughters fondly. "Let the fun and games begin." She turned towards Samuel, a twinkle in her eyes. "Organizing a wedding means all hands on deck. You will announce your engagement in the church, of course, but we will need you to deliver the invitations. Get the barn ready for all the guests."

He nodded. "Of course."

"Will I get married here or at your home, *Mamm?*" Judith asked.

Sadie exchanged a glance with her husband. "You decide, dear."

Ben grinned. "We shall keep with tradition. We will have the wedding at our home. Samuel and Judith must stay in the *dawdihaus* for the first few months of their marriage. There is enough space for Isaiah. Just as well we built a two-bedroom!"

Judith smiled at Samuel, remembering he had never married before. "Samuel, we need to fix a date for the wedding. As my future husband, the decision is yours."

"Hmm. Give me a moment to think about it."

"Don't take too long," Ben said dryly, grinning at him.

Samuel burst out laughing. "Point taken. I suggest we marry in October." He turned to Judith. "Does that give us enough time to organize the wedding?"

"That gives us just over two months," Judith said, looking at her mother with doubtful eyes. "Do you think that's possible?"

Sadie shook her head. "Rather have the wedding in early November. That gives us three months." She smiled at Samuel knowingly. "You better get lots of sleep in the months leading up to the wedding. With all the planning and ordering food and supplies, it gets hectic."

Judith put down her glass, turning to her mother. "I'm sure Mark wouldn't mind lending a hand in delivering the invitations."

"You better chat to him first," Samuel said gently. "He's got a lot on his plate already."

Judith laughed. "He told me he would be happy to help, earlier, so that is settled. Besides, we can spread the load over several weeks. The invitations don't have to be delivered all at once."

A few weeks later, Judith felt stressed and irritable. The same thing happened when she had planned her wedding to Isaac. Her mother was being rather bossy.

"The wedding invitations need to be delivered by the first week of September," Sadie said dogmatically.

Judith's brows knitted in consternation. "*Mamm*, we agreed that Samuel and Mark would handle the invitations over several weeks. I am sure it's fine that the guests get their invitations six weeks before. You are putting unnecessary pressure on them."

Her mother pursed her mouth. "You would rather have guests not turn up because they made other plans?"

Judith took a deep breath. "If it comes to that, *jah*. A few guests not being able to make it wouldn't be the end of the world."

Her mother clicked her tongue. "Don't put words in my mouth. I just want as many of your friends to be there as possible."

"I don't have three hundred friends, *Mamm*. I will tell my closest friends the date of our wedding the next time I see them."

"That's not the point! A wedding is to be celebrated by the community. We should try to ensure that as many of our neighbors and friends are there as possible. They are there as witnesses to your vows. And to give you and Samuel their blessing."

Judith would meet her mother's requests halfway for the sake of peace. "Could *Daed* help with delivering some of the wedding invitations? With his help, we could get them delivered in early September."

Her mother drew herself more upright, smiling. "That's a wonderful idea. Your father would love to be involved."

Judith hoped for her father's sake that her mother was right. "*Gut*. Could you please ask him if he could deliver about a hundred invitations?"

Her mother blinked, alarmed. "So many? Remember your *daed* is getting on in years. I was thinking he could help with about fifty."

Judith was thankful she knew how to control her temper or she might have said something she regretted. "Fifty would help." But not enough to get all the invitations delivered by her mother's deadline.

"Get the invitations delivered by the first week of September," her mother said, giving her a pointed stare. She drew herself up from her chair, stretching her shoulders. "Worked on a quilt last night. My back is aching."

Judith rose from her chair. "Sorry to hear that. I should be heading home. I better wake Isaiah now. If he sleeps any longer, he won't sleep tonight."

"Would you like me to babysit on Saturday?' her mother asked, pressing a hand on her arm.

Judith's earlier irritation towards her faded. "*Danke* for the offer. But there is no need. Samuel is taking us out for supper. He promised Isaiah a milkshake."

Her mother beamed. "Samuel is so *gut* to Isaiah. He already treats him like his *sohn*."

Judith felt a brief moment of heartache for Isaac never knowing his son. She was careful not to show it.

"*Jah*. And Isaiah adores him. Speaking of which, I better go wake him."

Her mother laughed. "He is probably going through a growth spurt. He will need new clothes for the wedding too."

Judith smiled at her words. She was probably right. She was told Isaiah was very like his uncle Mark at the same age. Today, Mark was well over six feet. Isaiah ate like a horse but her whole family had hearty appetites. Nowadays that was due to a fondness for the sociability of mealtime rather than a need for nourishment.

Judith had heeded her mother's advice about meal preparation. Isaiah was thriving on wholesome food rather than a diet of fast foods which many mothers gave their children nowadays. She and Samuel were taking a few day's break that week. Saturday would be the first time since Tuesday that they would be seeing each other.

The newly engaged couple had decided to do that because Isaiah was demanding more attention than Samuel could give during his working day. Also, Judith reasoned, if they were a courting couple who lived further apart they would have seen less of each other. She needed some time to herself too.

Judith was finding organizing a wedding, packing orders for clients, and billing them quite the juggling act. Being a blushing fiancée added another dimension to her life and one she was incredibly grateful for. She loved Samuel. Being able to love another man seemed like a miracle after losing her first husband.

After losing Isaac, if someone had told her that her heart could heal to some extent, Judith would have struggled to believe that. She would always remember Isaac. Honor his birthday. Remember their wedding day. Recall the love they shared. Hold onto special memories, like when she announced she was expecting their child.

But now she was looking forward to building a family with Samuel and Isaiah. Having a joyful family was more important to her than the farm. Although the farm was part of her identity now. She hoped to always be a farmer's wife. Have acres of land around her that she and her husband could pass on to Isaiah one day and other generations.

It was too early to say whether Isaiah would want to be a farmer. Not all Amish men followed in their father's footsteps. She would let her son choose his path one day. Judith chuckled. She was as much of a traditionalist as her mother. One of the things she enjoyed most about being Amish was that so many families continued their family traditions.

In Lancaster, the Amish surrounded themselves with families they had known since childhood. Besides being frowned upon, there was no room for pretense in a community rooted in family values and lending support to neighbors. Yet life wasn't idyllic. There were folk less welcoming to people who had left the community to return years later. Samuel had confided in her recently about his fears of coming home.

"The bishop advised me to ease into the community again when I first returned," Samuel said. He took the cup of steaming coffee that Judith handed him after lunch. He was having the rare treat of spending lunch with her at the farmhouse as a rainstorm was brewing.

"What did the bishop mean by that?"

"He told me to rather not join men's sports groups or activities until I received an invitation." He gave a wry laugh. "That didn't matter much. I arrived in the heart of winter and I got stuck into my job at the farm. I got an invitation in March to play bowls. I accepted. The rest as they say is history. No one has ever made any negative comments since I returned."

"I'm glad our community has made you feel welcome."

Samuel shrugged. "Maybe they did because I remained Amish although I left. I didn't abandon Amish customs. I have never courted an *Englisch* woman."

She nodded, happy about that too. "Are your aunt and uncle coming to our wedding?"

"*Jah*, they have accepted. They wouldn't miss it for the world!"

"Have they got a place to stay?"

"They will probably book into a local hotel."

"Why don't they rather stay in the farmhouse?"

Samuel's face lit up. "They would love that. *Danke*, Judith."

"*Lieb*, it will be our *haus* after we are married."

"*Jah*, but I'd like to make some improvements. Make it our home."

Judith prodded his arm, teasingly. "What needs improvement, Mister Fischer?"

"Well, let me see. I need to push the bathroom door to get it properly closed. Why is it like that anyway?"

"I was cleaning and I left a broom behind the door. I rushed to check on Isaiah after he scraped his knee. We returned to the bathroom. The broom had fallen sideways and got wedged behind the door, messing up the hinge."

"Oops. That's a bigger job than I thought. I will need to hire help to have the door rehung."

Judith kissed his cheek. "That would be wonderful. It annoys me the way it is. Anything else needs fixing?"

Samuel chuckled. "*Jah*, the porch roof leaks as I recall."

She giggled. "I don't usually sit there during a rainstorm. It was a *gut* excuse to have you stay longer after supper until we realized the rain wasn't going to stop soon."

"I got drenched walking from the *haus* to my buggy." Samuel gave her a cheeky grin. "Just as well we're getting married so you don't shoo me out into the rain to protect your reputation."

"You exaggerate! I lent you an umbrella."

"Which almost blew inside-out on the way to my buggy."

"Oh, Samuel-" Judith said softly. "I'm so glad you came back into my life."

He stared at her. "I never dreamed we would court again and marry. I was glad of the opportunity to help you. The more I got to know you, the more I wanted to court you. I had no idea how to handle the situation beyond taking it day by day. Joining you and Isaiah for supper gave me a glimmer of hope that you might welcome a relationship with me."

"I had fears to work through, too," Judith said softly. "I thought you might not want to court a woman with a child, even if you cared about her. I worried whether the community would consider me shallow for moving on so quickly after Isaac's death."

"The folk who know you well, and that's a *gut* number, know you were a faithful wife to Isaac. And you are a loving mother to Isaiah. I doubt anyone is speaking ill of you for courting me or marrying me."

"If they did, it wouldn't make an iota of difference to my feelings for you." *She loved him with all her heart.*

When they married in November, many guests told them it was one of the happiest weddings they had attended. May's remark that afternoon was especially meaningful.

"Judith, I was so sad for you when you lost Isaac," May whispered as they stood near the main table. "Everything was so difficult for you. Then having Isaiah prematurely and having to raise him alone. I wondered how on earth you would get through that awful period in your life." May smiled.

"Now I see you with Samuel, the joy on your faces. Now I know *Gott* can restore hope, even after the worst of times. *Gott* bless you and your marriage."

Judith stared at her sister, amazed. "That is one of the wisest things anyone has ever told me. *Danke*, sweetie pie." The sisters flung their arms around each other like they did when they were much younger, laughing.

"Like to join me in playing a game of skittles?" Samuel said, touching his wife's arm, his eyes filled with love.

"*Jah*, Mister Fischer," Judith said, breathless as he took her hand.

CHAPTER 9

*T*he following spring, six months after their wedding, the Fischer family was eating lunch on the porch. Judith had set up a table there for them and visitors to enjoy the sunshine. Isaiah stretched his arm towards the breadbasket.

Judith arched a brow. "Please may I have some more?"

Isaiah dropped his hand like he had touched a hot potato. "Sorry, *Mamm*."

Samuel and Judith smiled at each other. Samuel lifted the breadbasket, holding it near Isaiah.

"You may take another roll."

"*Danke, Daed*."

Samuel smiled at Judith, lifting the basket so

that the remaining rolls bounced. "Like another one?"

She giggled, taking one. "*Danke.*"

Samuel peered at Isaiah. "Could I have the last one?"

Isaiah smirked, his mouth full.

Samuel popped another roll on his plate. "*Danke* for a wonderful meal." Judith nodded while she buttered her bread, looking preoccupied for reasons beyond what she was doing. She clasped her hands to her face as if thankful. Samuel had never seen her look so serene. Or beautiful. Her skin glowed with good health.

Her cheeks seemed fuller. If she had put on weight, it suited her. Judith had lost a lot of weight in the two years of running the farm alone after Isaac's death. That was one of the things Samuel had noticed about her after so many years away.

"You look very pretty today," he said.

Judith laughed. "*Danke.*" She continued eating as if in a world of her own. Puzzled, Samuel studied her. She was quieter than usual. She seemed different, in a good way.

Judith looked up to find him watching her. "Why are you staring at me?"

"Admiring my wife," he said lazily, flattered that her cheeks flushed at his compliment.

Her meal finished, she dabbed her mouth with a serviette. "I have something to tell you and Isaiah," she said, looking at them with amusement. "I am pregnant."

Samuel gaped at her and then he stretched his hand to take hers. "You're having a *boppli*?" *Beyond marrying her, this was the happiest news he had ever had.*

Isaiah interrupted, his eyes as big as saucers. "When, *Mamm*?"

"In late November. I'm already two months pregnant."

Stroking his wife's hand, Samuel said, "I knew there was something different about you."

Judith laughed. "I'm glad I don't have morning sickness. I didn't tell you before because I wanted to be sure."

Isaiah leaned towards his mother. "I will be a *bruder*?"

"*Jah*, you will! You will be three years older than your *bruder* or *schweschder*."

"That's a lot," Isaiah said proudly, turning his head to smile at Samuel.

"We will be a *familye* of four," Samuel said,

amazed at how his life had changed for the better. A year ago, when he asked Judith to marry him, his mind had been focused on becoming her husband and a father to Isaiah. Now he would support her during her pregnancy. Marvel at the miracle of them having a baby. Seeing Judith's slender body change shape as their baby grew would be marvelous too.

"How are you feeling?" he asked. He would support his wife every step of the way. He would help her when she became tired. Judith let go of his hand to take a sip of water.

"I feel marvelous except for sudden exhaustion after supper. That is normal. My energy will return in a few weeks."

Samuel peered at her. "I must take you to the doctor for a check-up."

"We can wait another month," she said with the air of a woman who had been pregnant before.

"We shall do no such thing," Samuel said firmly. "Please make an appointment. The sooner the better. The doctor can check your blood pressure. The baby's heartbeat. Check you aren't anemic. Confirm the baby's birth date too."

Judith raised her brows. "Fine, I shall make an

appointment. I'd like to have our *boppli* at home this time if possible."

Isaiah peered at her. "Was I born in a hospital?"

Judith smiled at him. "You arrived a few weeks early. I was glad you were healthy when you were born. You gave such a loud cry, I knew you were strong."

"Why did I cry?" Isaiah asked, appearing concerned by that fact. Judith was quiet, at a loss for words as she remembered his birth. She had mixed feelings. Incredible joy at her son's birth. But sadness over losing Isaac. Noticing Judith's tear-filled eyes, Samuel leaned towards Isaiah.

"*Bopplin* cry when they are born. They gulp air. Crying expands their lungs and clears their chest. They also cry because they are suddenly in a new place, filled with people. That's why a *mamm* needs to hold her *boppli* close so they feel safe."

Isaiah's eyes were earnest. "Can I see the *boppli* when it is born?"

Judith smiled. "*Jah*, you can see your little *bruder* or *schweschder* after they are born."

"Can I go play at my cousins' this week?" Isaiah asked suddenly.

Judith smiled knowingly. "*Jah*, you can, if they

are home on Saturday. Do you want to tell them you are going to be a big *bruder*?"

Isaiah beamed. "*Jah, Mamm.*"

On Saturday, Samuel stayed at the farm while Judith visited Mark and his family. An excited Isaiah waved at him from the seat next to his mother. Judith blew him a kiss. She regularly drove the buggy herself on Saturdays, saving Samuel from making a trip when he had work to do.

"Have a *gut* visit!" he called. Samuel could tell Isaiah was bursting to tell his cousins that he was going to have a brother or sister soon. He smiled, imagining how his brother-in-law and Ruby

would react to the announcement. Judith's parents would be incredibly happy. He knew that because Sadie had told him she would be happy to be a grandmother again.

Samuel had built up quite an enterprise on the farm. He took a seat on the comfortable chair he had treated himself to. He opened the leather-bound notebook in which he made laborious notes every week. He logged his wholesale nursery sales there, and he recorded the names of plants that had flourished beyond his expectations.

He added up the last quarter's sales and his eyes

widened. He double-checked his calculations. He was set to quadruple his wholesale nursery output by the next growing season. *Their child would be born by then.* He bent his head, uttering a silent prayer of gratitude for help unseen and God's provision.

Now he could truly understand that verse, *a peace that surpasseth all understanding.* The incredible thing was how the very thing that he had always struggled with – writing – was becoming easier. He had always been quick to work out sums and see the logical answer to a problem. But writing had always presented a challenge. Writing exercises had once caused him such anxiety that his hands shook whenever he picked up a pen to do a test at school.

Judith had spent several evenings with him that week, going over words that he struggled to spell and write. Samuel still had to concentrate on each word but he found the sentences forming with greater ease. Rather than his words trailing off in unfinished sentences and rather than words being jumbled. Now he could understand what he had written.

He could now write with a clarity of expression that he would never have thought possible. His incredible wife had amazed him with her patience the previous evening. *A Friday!* They had gone over some words multiple times. After Samuel had finally conquered over twenty words he had always struggled to write, he drew his arms around Judith as they sat on the couch together.

"I love you," he murmured.

Judith rested her head on his shoulder, taking his hand. "I love you, too."

Samuel bent his head to kiss her forehead. "You know that corny expression, you make me want to be a better *mann?*"

She lifted her head, smiling. "Sure."

"You make me want to be a better *mann.* I never dreamed I would choose to spend a Friday evening with my wonderful wife, admitting how confused writing and reading make me feel. Owning up to my weakness."

She stared at him, frowning. "You are far from weak. It takes courage to admit that you need help. I was glad to help you. You are bright, Samuel. No one is *gut* at everything."

He chuckled. "I've met a few people who seem to be."

"Perhaps they struggle with something you aren't aware of."

"Like what?"

"Maybe they have a sweet tooth or a short temper. Maybe they don't like people knowing they aren't as perfect as they seem. Maybe they can't sleep at night."

"You never fail to amaze me," he murmured, caressing her hand. "You lost your first husband, yet here you are, boosting my morale."

"*Danke*."

That morning, before she left, Judith suggested that he check his sales from the last quarter. She had noticed how many more deliveries she had arranged in recent months. Now, staring at the profits from that quarter, Samuel knew his business was on a firm foundation.

His faith in God helped him every day. Even with his growing knowledge of horticulture and propagation, bugs could get into the plants. Ruin his plans. Unseasonably dry weather had hampered the chances of his fruit trees growing much that year.

Yet, overall, the good periods far outweighed any setbacks. As long as he persevered. Kept on planting, watering, and tending tiny shoots like his life depended on them growing. In a way, nurturing his plants nourished his soul. Beyond his love for Judith and Isaiah and his aunt and uncle, there was little to rival the peace that came from seeing a seed germinate, a cutting take root and a plant grow well over three feet.

The success of the past year wasn't all his doing. Judith helped with the nursery. She checked leaves for spots and bugs. She immediately told him if she noticed a plant's leaves wilting. She was quick to notice such things. Samuel's days were often wrapped up in securing new orders and loading plants on the truck that came past the farm once a week.

Samuel took several hours planning a call sheet, determined to make deliveries as profitable as possible. He was glad to help Judith with the produce side of the farm. He handled the plowing and the bulk of the planting. Judith insisted that she plant some of the crops.

"Mind telling me why?" Samuel asked good-naturedly after he told her a field was ready for planting.

Judith hesitated. "You might think me silly."

He grinned. "Try me."

She stared at him, hesitant. "I like to feel the earth between my fingers and I say a prayer."

"Why would I think that silly?"

"And I like to also plant the crop. Not just rely on you."

Samuel's next question was gentle. "Are you scared to depend on me entirely? In case something should happen to me?"

Her mouth trembled. "How did you know that?"

He hugged her close, gazing towards the fields. "You looked so vulnerable." He pulled apart to stare at her. "Please let me plant an entire field for you the next time. You are the one bringing the crops to life with your watering program and crop rotation.

"You have done so well. Why not accept a helping hand? Take a rest when you can." He touched her tummy gently. "You will soon have a baby to care for. You won't be able to plant in the months immediately following the baby's birth."

She threw her head back and laughed. "Says who!"

He gave her a rueful smile. "Such a determined woman, my wife."

"The *boppli* can be in a pram while I work in the field," Judith said firmly.

"We shall see about that," Samuel said. He

wasn't convinced that it was a wise idea for her to do physical work so soon after having a baby.

"I'm strong!" she said, giggling.

"So I have gathered." Samuel kissed her. "No doubt about that."

"Do you dislike me being so outspoken?" she asked, quieter.

"Not at all. I just want to make sure you do what's best for you and our *boppli*."

"That's sweet."

"I prefer it when you tell me I'm strong," he teased.

When Judith returned that afternoon, Samuel laughed as he saw her approach the door, laden with containers.

"What's all that?" he asked.

"Ruby blessed us with a batch of biscuits. Then I went to my parents. My mother was so excited at hearing the news that she rushed off to tell my father who was doing woodwork. Then they both insisted they take us out for *kaffe*. I brought a take-away slice of cake for you."

"Now, that is sweet," Samuel said, kissing her.

CHAPTER 10

"Give a few more pushes," the midwife said with the stoic acceptance of one who had helped many mothers give birth. With what little energy she had left to muster, Judith took a deep breath and pushed.

"Almost there," Margaret, the midwife announced. Judith lay back against the pillow, heaving from the effort, her face clammy with perspiration. At one awful stage, she had felt like asking for a prescription drug to alleviate her pain. Then she thought of Samuel waiting outside, worried about her and their baby.

She didn't want to disappoint him. Their baby would be born at home as she had hoped and prayed. The door opened several inches. Samuel stuck his head in the room.

"Please tell me everything is fine," he said, his voice tight with concern.

"Judith is doing well," the midwife said. "I will call you as soon as the *boppli* is born."

"Danke." Samuel clicked the door closed. Judith imagined him pacing up and down.

"Push again," the midwife urged.

"Argh," Judith groaned as the baby's head crowned.

The midwife chuckled. "Almost there. One more push. You can do it."

Judith pushed for all she was worth, her energy spent. She peered at the golden-headed baby the midwife was cleaning. The baby gave a lusty cry, her eyes squished closed, her cheeks rosy.

Judith smiled as Samuel rushed to her side, peering at her anxiously.

"How are you feeling?" he asked.

"Tired." She turned her head, smiling at him. "Happy we have a *boppli*. Glad you are here."

The midwife wrapped the baby in a pink blanket. "You have a wonderful little girl. Are you ready to hold her?" Judith nodded, too overcome with joy to speak. She and Samuel gazed at their baby and then at each other, their eyes glistening with tears.

"*Hallo*, Mimi," Samuel whispered, touching the baby's hand. Her hand curled around his fingers. Her crying stopped as if his touch had soothed her.

Judith laughed. "Would you like to hold her?"

Samuel nodded. "*Jah*." He carefully took the golden-haired little girl, cradling her in his arms. "*Hallo*, Mimi. I am your Papa, Samuel. Your *Mamm* and I promise to love and cherish you."

"I will leave you alone," the midwife said softly. "Can I let Isaiah in the room now?"

Judith's eyes softened. "*Jah, danke.* Thanks for helping me and the *boppli*." Isaiah entered the room, making a beeline for his mother's bed. He stared at the baby in awe and then at his mother.

"*Hallo*, sweetie pie," Judith said tiredly, gazing at him from her bed.

"*Hallo, Mamm*," he whispered as if she was the most marvelous mother for bringing his sister into the world.

Samuel lowered the baby so Isaiah could see her better. "Meet your little *schweschder*, Mimi."

"*Hallo*, Mimi." Isaiah stared at her intensely. He glanced at Samuel, smiling. "She is tiny!"

"*Jah*, and she's as *gut* as gold. She stopped crying when I picked her up."

Judith touched Samuel's sleeve. "Can I hold her again, *Liebe*?"

He chuckled, handing her their baby with utmost care. "Mimi says *hallo*."

Judith giggled. "*Hallo*, Mimi," she whispered tenderly. "Welcome to our *familye*. Your big *bruder* can hold you when you are a bit older."

Mimi shifted in her arms, quiet. Her eyes opened. She squinted in the light, blinking as she adjusted to the glare, her gaze fixed on her mother. Judith felt like her heart had melted as their eyes connected.

"She has the loveliest eyes," Judith murmured. "*Kumm* closer, you two."

"Want a closer look?" Samuel asked Isaiah.

Isaiah nodded. "Uh-huh."

Samuel picked Isaiah up so he could admire the new addition to their family too. "Looks like she has your eyes," he said, smiling at his wife. "Do you want water?"

"*Jah, danke.* I am very thirsty."

Margaret returned, carrying a glass of water. "For you." She put it on the bedside table beside Judith.

Samuel laughed. "I was just going to fetch some."

Margaret gave a hearty laugh. "You catch on quick." She turned her attention to Judith. "How are you feeling, my dear?"

"I'm thirsty. *Danke.*"

Margaret spoke with authority, "I will hold the *boppli* while you drink your water. Drink all of it. You need to feed the baby. The water will help bring on the milk." Margaret fussed with Judith's pillow, making her more comfortable.

Judith sat up, draining the glass of water. "That's better!" She smiled at Samuel, noticing that he was still holding Isaiah. He was such a caring father. She felt sure he would soon get the hang of having a baby in the house. They would all have to adjust their routine.

Samuel shifted on his feet as if he felt awkward being there. "I will check on you later, *Liebe.*"

Judith smiled at her husband and Isaiah. "Love you both."

The nurse stepped forward, peering at Judith. "You must feed the *boppli* now."

Samuel put Isaiah down. The three-year-old gave his mother a lingering look as he left the room, reluctant to leave her and his little sister.

Mimi drank thirstily. Judith was relieved she had enough milk. Some mothers struggled at first because they were tired. She felt such a strong bond with her baby already as she watched her nestle against her, her eyes closed tight again.

"I'm sure you would like a rest now," Margaret said.

"I would love a nap," Judith murmured, her eyes fixed on Mimi.

The midwife gave her an approving smile. "*Gut.* I will take the baby to Samuel. He can hold her for a while. Mimi looks like she is about to nod off any minute, so he should manage fine." Judith laughed. *A newborn baby took some getting used to, but what a blessing.*

MIMI WAS ALREADY three months old. Judith had no worries about Isaiah getting on with the new and lively addition to their household. Isaiah was besotted with his baby sister. He had taken on the role of tutor, mentor, and bodyguard. He drew the line at changing diapers though.

"Mimi, clap hands for me?" Isaiah asked, tickling her chin. Mimi gurgled, her podgy hands stretching to be picked up. Isaiah wasn't allowed to pick her up yet. Judith had promised he could when he turned four, and only when she said so. She was clear about that.

Isaiah was proving to be a great help. Mimi enjoyed all the attention he gave her. When Judith made supper for the family, Mimi sat in her high chair, playing with her rattle and communicating in her special way with her brother. Isaiah would show off his drawing skills at the table alongside her.

Judith scrutinized her son's latest drawing, surprised at the detail. "That's a cute picture."

"Can you see who it is?" he asked, frowning with concentration as he colored with a crayon.

"It's Mimi. I recognized her chubby cheeks."

Isaiah looked up. "Cool!" He had picked up that word from his cousins. He used it several times a day. Judith was beginning to think Mimi's first word might be cool.

Judith pressed a hand on Isaiah's shoulder, making him look up. "When you are done, could I put the picture on display? It's lovely!"

He shrugged. "If you like."

Samuel was still at his nursery which he had named *Samuel's Love Judith Nursery*. When he suggested the name, a few weeks back, Judith had laughed.

"You're joking."

"*Nee*, I'm not. It's a catchy name." He grinned. "Anyway, it's too late if you don't like it. I'm having a signpost made. I'm planning to start inviting folk to visit the nursery later this year. Give talks every so often."

Judith laughed. "Just as well I like the name." It was no wonder the wholesale nursery was booming. Samuel had new ideas all the time. His customers showed their appreciation by placing bigger orders and sending referrals their way. Samuel even held a lucky draw twice a year, where the winner won a tree if they spent a certain amount at the nursery.

Judith thought it wonderful that a man who had once feared ridicule for struggling with reading was becoming known as one of the sharpest businesspeople around. Samuel never bragged about his success. But he had developed a fantastic reputation for giving value for money. He cared about his customers. The reach of both businesses had extended way beyond their expectations.

Judith had hired help on the produce side. She

now supplied retailers who collected fruit and vegetables from the farm. She was exceedingly happy about that. It was blissful not having to get up at the crack of dawn to take her stock to the market. She still rose early to feed Mimi, but sitting in a chair with her baby in her arms was entirely different from loading the buggy.

She let Isaiah sleep in a little later than usual on Saturdays so he was benefitting from their success too. Her eyes rested on her three-year-old, remembering her panic that day a year ago when he had wandered off at the farmer's market. Judith was settled and far happier now. She was thankful to be able to enjoy her days again.

Mimi smacked her rattle on the edge of her high chair. Judith whirled around to see her giving her daddy a big smile.

Samuel laughed. "Someone's happy to see me."

"So am I!" Judith said holding up her face for a kiss.

He kissed her. "I'm a lucky *mann*!"

Isaiah jumped up from his chair. "Look, Daed. It's Mimi."

"I think his picture is rather *gut*," Judith said, careful not to praise too much.

"Let's see that," Samuel said, taking the picture

and studying it. "That is a *gut* likeness of Mimi."

"*Danke, Daed.*" Isaiah stuck the picture on the cooler, using the magnet his mother always left there, to stick on reminder notes for shopping.

Samuel gazed at Judith. "I was thinking we should have a holiday later this year. Mimi should almost be walking by then. We can take the stroller. Isaiah and I can ride horses. Catch fish."

"I love the idea. But it will still be cold then. Let's rather wait until spring."

"We can do that." Samuel grinned. "But let's spend a weekend away as a *familye* before then. Imagine ordering meals for a change instead of doing all the cooking. And always cleaning up after Mimi."

"I help with Mimi," Isaiah mumbled.

Samuel ruffled his hair. "*Jah*, you help a lot. Mimi is lucky to have a *bruder* like you. But I was thinking more of your mother. She could do with a few days off." Judith tilted her head, thinking how much she had to be grateful for.

"You know what? I am happy bustling around at home, working on the farm, as long as the three of you are around." She was a contented woman. She had more to be thankful for than many people dreamed of.

She had fought through her sorrow. Judith still had days when she remembered something Isaac had said or they had shared, and her eyes would fill with sudden tears. Now she let that memory comfort her. Her life was here on the farm with the family she loved.

Samuel was a wonderful husband. She loved him with all her heart. His sense of humor calmed her when she needed to take a step back. Sometimes a person just needed to see things from a different perspective to feel better.

Her husband peered at the still-bubbling pot. "Could we possibly save carrot soup for tomorrow night? I've got a hankering for pizza. The garlic not so much."

Judith laughed. "We can do that. That sounds like fun. The garlic not so much."

"Garlic keeps the bugs away."

Judith poked his arm. "Haha. Just give me ten minutes to get ready."

"You already look beautiful, *Lieb*."

"*Danke*. But I'd like to change into a fresh dress. Mimi's sticky hands left a mark on my skirt."

"Did she have candy?" Isaiah asked, sounding wistful.

"*Nee*, she just drooled milk on my skirt."

Isaiah shuddered. "Ew!"

Judith soon returned, wearing the purple dress she had worn on her wedding day.

Samuel stared at her as if entranced. "Thanks for marrying me."

"Go wash your hands, Isaiah," Judith said quietly. Her son scooted off, a spring in his step.

Judith smiled at Samuel. "Thanks for being brave enough to help me on the farm. Becoming my best friend."

Samuel wrapped his arms around her, pulling her close. "I had no idea what to expect but I wanted to help you. See you again."

"It's amazing because we all helped each other. Isaiah needed a father. You made me believe in love again."

Mimi bashed her rattle. "Da da," she cooed.

"Did she say that?" Samuel asked, incredulous. "Don't babies usually start talking much later?"

Judith laughed as she picked up their little girl. "Not our Mimi."

"I taught her to say da da," Isaiah said proudly.

Samuel grinned. "I believe you! Let's go get a pizza to celebrate."

Judith was convinced that being such a happy family called for a celebration too. "Let's!"

STAY IN TOUCH

Join my super fans and become the very first to hear about new releases, special offers and free books. Sign up below.

CLICK HERE TO BE THE FIRST TO KNOW

ALSO BY HANNAH SCHROCK

The Amish Girl Who Lives Next Door

In a world divided by tradition and progress, the Amish Lehman family collide with their new English neighbors, the Andersons. The chasm isn't just a fence, it's a wall of age-old beliefs and values.

Caught in this whirlwind, nineteen-year-old Sarah Lehman unexpectedly falls for the forbidden Joe Anderson, the handsome son from next door.

Charmed by Sarah's strength, Joe can't resist the pull between them. Despite familial disapproval and social scorn, their bond deepens, fortified by clandestine encounters and the support of an unlikely ally.

As Sara's loyalties to her faith and community are tested, Joe grapples with a life-altering decision - a choice that could forever change their fates. But he was oblivious to the impending storm of heartache his decision may unleash.

Amidst stark differences and brewing tension, can their extraordinary love weather the storm? Can the fence that separates them be destroyed so their destinies can lie together?

DOWNLOAD NOW